The Six-Pointed Star

Establecimento Prisonal de Lisboa

The entrance to the "Six-Pointed Star"

The Six-Pointed Star
(A estrela de seis pontas)

MANUEL TIAGO
(Álvaro Cunhal)

Translated and with a foreword by
Eric A. Gordon

INTERNATIONAL PUBLISHERS
New York

Library of Congress Cataloging-in-Publication Data

Names: Tiago, Manuel, author. | Gordon, Eric A., 1945- translator.
Title: The six-pointed star = (A estrela de seis pontas) / Manuel Tiago
  (Álvaro Cunhal) ; translated and with a foreword by Eric A. Gordon.
Other titles: Estrela de seis pontas. English
Description: First English language edition. | New York : International
  Publishers, 2020. | Summary: "Set in a Portuguese prison during the
  fascist era, this book is a composite tapestry of a place, a time, and a
  shifting population of 500 men. Almost any reader will be able to
  identify moments in their own lives when they were just this far away
  from committing a crime, or wanting to, and ending up as these men did.
  However many reasons there may be why people commit crimes, even heinous
  ones, prison does not cancel a person's humanity. That may be in itself
  the single most important 'message' the book is trying to communicate"—
  Provided by publisher.
Identifiers: LCCN 2020044810 (print) | LCCN 2020044811 (ebook) | ISBN
  9780717808359 (paperback) | ISBN 9780717808366 (mobi) | ISBN
  9780717808373 (epub)
Classification: LCC PQ9282.I23 E713 2020 (print) | LCC PQ9282.I23 (ebook)
  | DDC 869.3/42—dc23
LC record available at https://lccn.loc.gov/2020044810
LC ebook record available at https://lccn.loc.gov/2020044811

ISBN 10: 0-7178-0835-1   ISBN 13: 978-0-7178-0835-9
Typeset by Amnet Systems, Chennai, India

WITH THE SUPPORT OF THE GENERAL
DIRECTORATE FOR BOOKS,
ARCHIVES AND LIBRARIES/DGLAB AND
CAMÕES, INSTITUTO DA
COOPERAÇÃO E DA LÍNGUA I.P./
CAMÕES I.P. –PORTUGAL

Also available from International Publishers
in its series of fictional works by
Manuel Tiago

Five Days, Five Nights

Table of Contents

Foreword

By Eric A. Gordon

As noted in the author biography, Álvaro Cunhal himself spent 11 years in the Portuguese prison system for his Communist Party activism and leadership, much of that time in strict isolation in a cell at the Fort of Peniche, a couple of hours' drive up the coast from Lisbon.

It is abundantly clear that the author derived much of his raw material for this book about prison life from the years he himself spent in the clutches of the Portuguese fascist state, and from other actual cases with which the author was personally acquainted or knew of. The story of the Communist who dies of starvation is of course presented within a work of fiction, but is the actual story of Militão Ribeiro, who died in the Lisbon Penitentiary on January 2, 1950 (weighing 37 kilos!). Militão needed urgent medical assistance and went on hunger strike to protest against its denial by the prison authorities. Historians have written about this comrade: http://www.avante.pt/pt/2404/temas/157650/Sabes-como-mo rreu--o-valente-Militão.htm.

Comrades of Cunhal's generation would not likely be capable of identifying any of the other characters portrayed in *The Six-Pointed Star*, though in other writings that follow in this series devoted to the work of "Manuel Tiago," many more such parallels between life and art might be more salient. Most of the characters depicted in this novelistic memoir of prison life had been convicted for other types of crimes—violent, mostly—not typically fitting the profile of a political prisoner.

Cunhal was arrested (together with Militão Ribeiro and Sofia Ferreira) on March 25, 1949. He was imprisoned in the (six-pointed) Lisbon Penitentiary from April 1949 until July 27, 1956. He was kept incommunicado for 14 months. Later, due to his poor health (a consequence of the eight years spent clandestinely prior to his arrest, plus the 14 months incommunicado), he was transferred to the infirmary. The conditions being less harsh, it was here that he met and came to know about the hundreds of common prisoners he fictionally describes in the novel.

On July 27, 1956, Cunhal was transferred to the Fort of Peniche, from which he escaped, with nine other comrades, on January 3, 1960—one of the most spectacular and daring escapes in the history of the world communist movement. Formally, his prison term was already over. But he had also been condemned to arbitrary "security measures," which allowed for successive extensions of six months to three years, indefinitely, at the will of the PIDE, the political police.

But it is not necessary to be able to pair up Tiago's pen-portraits with actual personages to be able to appreciate the gritty realism of this work. Many writers, in print, theater, film and television, have taken up the subject of prison (some from personal experience) and created a whole library devoted to this genre. My own feeling—I am prejudiced, of course—is that *The Six-Pointed Star*, now available to a wider English-language readership, will join the select company of great books on this theme.

"To know each man there," Tiago writes, "it's not enough to say he killed, robbed, assaulted, defrauded or raped. It's been said that there aren't crimes, just criminals. Many who committed crimes could well have spent their whole lives without doing them."

In this composite tapestry of a place, a time, and a shifting population of 500 men, almost any reader will be able to identify moments in their own lives when they were just *this far away* from committing a crime, or wanting to, and ending up as these men did. However many reasons there may be why people commit crimes, even heinous ones, prison does not cancel a person's humanity. That may be in itself the single most important "message" the book is trying to communicate.

Silvino is one of the book's most engaging characters, a man intently curious about life who clearly has some formal education. As an example of his close examination of nature, Tiago writes, "He discovered that the African winged ant, with brown stripes on its back, would flutter close to the ground until finding a fat caterpillar in the roots of a plant. It would then go some distance to find a hiding place, come back and grab the caterpillar with unsuspected force, happily dig a hole, inject its eggs into the caterpillar's body, place the caterpillar in the hole, and cover and disguise the hole in an artful work of construction worthy of a licensed engineer or architect."

Others in this volume, too, will show astounding problem-solving ingenuity, including some who nearly succeeded in escaping, and one who did. That kind of practical intelligence, analyzing the nature of phenomena and deriving appropriate conclusions, is an incalculable necessity if a person—or a society as a whole—wants to evolve from where they are now to the next stage.

Tiago opens and closes his memoir-novel on the outside of the prison. Throughout are pointers to his idea that life on the inside mirrors that on the outside, and vice versa. If theft, corruption, rape, sadism, violence, class privilege, vanity, caring, friendship, compassion and love and all the other qualities that make humans human exist on the outside, well, they exist too on the inside.

Our philosopher Silvino again: "You look out at space and you ask yourself, how does it end? Where does it end? You look at a fly and you say, This is only what it is, it's practically nothing, it ends here. I've thought a lot and I think that's wrong. The world that's inside the tiniest being is as immense as the world outside. First, because the more you divide, there'll always be more you can divide, and second, the more you add, there'll always be more you can add."

As a committed writer on the left, Cunhal appreciated that the successful development of each individual human being is important in equal measure with the success of the larger community or nation, and that they are interdependent. As a panoramic view of prison life, with many close-ups on any number of unique characters, Cunhal's treatment inherently asks whether such a balanced outcome is even possible under capitalist conditions, much less the fascist society he is describing.

I would like to express profound appreciation for their time and talent to Bill Gregory, Francisco Melo, Frederic A. Gordon, Isaura Arez, John Mueter, José Oliveria, Luciana Assini, Michael Cytrynowicz, Robert N. Miller, Ruth Judkowitz, Steve Johnson, and Vilmar Teixeira. Their highly generous and valuable contributions and suggestions helped to make this translation glow with passion and vitality.

Finally, I would like to extend a very belated thanks to my first Portuguese teacher, the late Prof. Malcolm C. Batchelor of Yale University, who instilled in me an enduring love for the language. If by chance another of his students should happen upon these words, I know they will share my profound feeling of debt.

The Six-Pointed Star

The Six-Pointed Star

By Manuel Tiago
Translated by Eric A. Gordon

ALONG the promenade, on a street animated by vehicle and pedestrian commotion, an eye-catching façade rose up with handsome towers and numerous windows framed in white stone. The building spread out on both sides with high walls outlined by battlements of the same stone.

At first glance, you'd say it was the ancient castle of a great lord, suggesting, on the other side of the walls, the refreshing, cool shade of parks and gardens. A few details, however, clashed with that first impression. The windows, even though elegantly scalloped, were grated, and the heavy, monumental architecture manifested a suspect grandiosity. Whoever stopped to look would certainly wonder: What is this?

Difficult to guess.

On the other side of the graceful architecture and walls that faced onto the street, a panoramic view revealed something else. Stemming out from a central tower crowned by a carved cupola, six monstrous buildings stretched in six directions in the shape of a star. Monstrous indeed. Each one was eighty meters long and four stories high, pocked by dozens of grated peepholes. Down below, between the buildings, were vast, deserted asphalt triangles. Around the six buildings and the triangular spaces, enclosing them from point to point, sat a row of low barracks that only at one point opened onto a vegetable garden. Over there, atop a high wall, rose a long, narrow garden bordered by a long house on the ground level, also marked by a succession of small grated windows. Farther out, like a ring constricting the immense complex, lay a deep moat and a high wall with barbed wire suspended across the top, with numerous sentry boxes situated every few meters.

Such was the six-pointed star viewed from outside.

Inside, starting from the spacious rotunda underneath the central tower and separated from it by heavy grilled gates, the interior

3

spaces of the star's six wings opened up with the grandeur and echo of a cathedral nave. Inside each wing, on both sides, ran rows of metal-plate doors from the rotunda out to the point. Up above were first- and second-tier iron balconies with more plated doors. On each floor, in the middle of the wings, narrow iron bridges linked the balconies of one side to the other.

Such was the first view of the six-pointed star observed from the inside.

Five hundred cells, five hundred prisoners

Five hundred cells and five hundred prisoners, locked in long-term incarceration. For many—in prison jargon—until they depart "wrapped up in a topcoat of planks." Five, ten, fifteen, twenty or more years, most of the time secured in a cell, a rectangle two meters by four, lit by a tiny grated window beneath the ceiling that the prisoner cannot see out of. A cement floor, a narrow iron bed, the table, a surface seventy by forty centimeters covered with zinc and suspended from the wall. A stool with a minuscule seat. A pail for the necessities. True luxury: A metal basin with running water, the tap open during the first minutes of the day to wipe your face and a few minutes after meals to clean your mess kit.

Sicknesses, deaths, fights, lamentations, protests, revolts, punishments, and the replacement of the interned—so slowly that it is only perceptible over the span of years. Faces seen no more after lengthy periods of being part of the living physiognomy of the prison population. New faces that show up with many years ahead of them to spend there.

In truth, in this creeping, endless intermission of time, every day looks on the surface just like all the other days. Schedule, routine and ritual. Dirty chestnut-colored uniforms and caps with numbers stamped in white. And the strident whistles, the lineups and the roll call, the processions going and coming from the workshops, the metallic clanging of gates, the dry shuffle of slippers and clogs on the cement, the racket of iron grates and locks and bolts, the scurrying about with trays distributing meals, the cross-echoes in the immense empty space in the wings, the stink from emptying the waste pails into the nauseating discharge drains, the smell of disinfectant, and—the stench of all stenches in the opinion of some—the moldy odor of kale soup and fish fried in rancid oil when they uncovered the meal trays. So it went, day after day, week after week, month after month, year after year. For many, the rest of their lives.

This is not the world that passersby on the street out front could imagine, looking at the noble, fortified façade with towers of white stone hinting—beyond the walls topped by stately battlements—at cool parks and gardens.

Recreation

Circling all around, or conversing in groups of varying size, some standing, others isolating themselves, in different ways the prisoners spent their recreation hour in one of the triangular yards crammed into the ground floor of the immense, gloomy walls of the wings. Against the dirty chestnut blur of the uniforms and caps, the inmate numbers stood out, branded in white ink. The cold, humid autumn had arrived, and many of the prisoners gathered their collars and made brusque gestures, slapping their arms to warm up.

Among the prisoners who strolled in the yard that day, Nero was the most visible for his stature and corpulence. He was renowned for his imposing physique, but even more for his fierce reputation. Standing alongside others, he listened to them attentively, serenely, and expressionlessly. Once in a while, he'd surprise them with sudden explosions of belly laughs, and no one understood what tickled his merriment.

The arrogant prisoner 509 also circulated, showing off his authority. No one got involved with him.

In a group with several others, shivering Old Lady-Killer sat cowering on the ground, burying his nose deep into his collar. He spoke little, and as he appeared a semi-imbecile, some engaged with him only to mock.

The tubercular Silvino, lean and agile, who had returned to the wing yet another time after one of his frequent stays in the infirmary, walked up and down the yard. Sometimes he paused to gesticulate strangely. He'd impulsively pick something up from the ground and run to the sunlit workshop barracks wall to inspect it.

Little Friar, so called because he had attended a seminary, moved in disjointed, tenuous little steps, his palms together and his lips moving in unintelligible murmuring.

Tony, condemned for assault and rape, was known for his blond head of hair, his distracted glance, and youthful, mischievous attitude. He walked alone and quickly, from one side to the other, warming up on the march.

Epileptic Serpentina, tall and gangly like a crane, friendly and easy to converse with, spoke to one and all.

Fat, flabby Catalan also strolled alone. He was sentenced for swindling many thousands of *contos*. A single *conto* was a thousand *escudos*! Although known for his long catalogue of frauds, he did not consider himself a criminal, but merely an intelligent man who knew he was more intelligent than others.

In one corner of the yard, Augusto the prison gardener and 402 were calmly conversing. They had both been there several years and had become friends. They had only lately entered their thirties, but remained optimistic in the face of much time yet to serve. Augusto hailed from the mountains of Trás-os-Montes, condemned for a bloody crime. He spoke to everyone and was sought out by many who needed to get something off their chest or ask advice. 402 was a sailor. His case took place in a bar at Cais do Sodré. He defended himself in a fight, killed someone, and was sentenced to many years.

On that day, Augusto and 402 were exchanging ideas about the possibility or impossibility of escape. There was no memory of any prisoner who had succeeded in escaping. People remembered one time a long while back, when two guys failed, but only narrowly. In a fastidious, years-long labor of careful investigation and observation, they had scoured corridors and annexes, evaded the guards' vigilance, descended to the sub-basements, opened doors, cut grates, and discovered how to access the sewers. Finally, at a given day and hour, they entered the sewer until they found an exit. After many hours in that pigsty of slime and excrement, light from a crack in a sewer grate came into view above them. They clambered toward it and exited onto a busy street. In their state, drenched in shit and emanating an unmistakably foul smell, where could they go? Amidst the shock of the pedestrians, they ran around aimlessly. Farther on, they turned themselves in to a gentle, but surprised policeman on duty.

Augusto and 402 knew this story. As they spoke, they imagined various escape schemes. Augusto showed no inclination toward considering any such ideas.

To the contrary, 402, vigorous and agile like the seaman he always was, could think of nothing else. "One day you're going to come wanting to talk with me, and I won't be here."

As Augusto gestured incredulously, 402 added in a confident voice, "You'll see!"

The Silent Hour

The silent hour has a physical existence. It's announced, it advances and diffuses, invading the cells, importing with it a damp, heavy, sepulchral anguish. The prisoners are all gathered in, and one by one the metal-plated cell doors slam closed in the grim cadence of lockers and bolts. In the first minutes of everyone getting settled on his pallet, the clamor of voices shouting here and there, and the monologues of those talking to themselves, can still be heard.

Then the noise gradually dies out, and mysterious prayers become more spaced out and distinct.

A weak, imploring voice, almost sobbing, spreads throughout the wing.

"Forgive me, Lord, for my sins! Pardon me for the evil I've done! Forgive me!"

Everyone recognizes the Old Man's voice.

It's also the chosen moment for another, 210, in his loud voice, to recite the punishment already served and the punishment yet to come.

"Six years, eight months and twenty days have passed; still remaining sixteen years, three months and two days."

It was like that every nightfall the several years since he's been here.

From undefined places, isolated shouts can be heard dying off in the distance, indeterminate scraping sounds and severe, hollow coughing. From deep in the basement comes the echo of muffled, useless protests of some prisoner punished in isolation. Little by little, the sounds evaporate in the ample spaciousness and the somber atmosphere of the wings.

Before the almost complete silence settles in, once more the passionate but feeble, imploring plea resounds through the air. "Forgive me, Lord! Forgive me!"

Then nothing more. Everything seems to stop until the cold awakening the following morning. The immense complex of buildings in the star doesn't house hundreds of lives. Rather, you could say, it is the gigantic tomb of hundreds buried alive.

A Bandit from Alentejo

Garino was one of Augusto the gardener's best friends. He knew a lot, spoke well, and discoursed with discernment about whatever came up for consideration. When he said he was illiterate, no one hearing him would believe it. He came here some years back, and still he hadn't reached the age of thirty. He was a calm fellow from Alentejo who generally spoke in low, hesitant tones, almost always with veiled irony. He only got riled up when someone really tested his limits.

Those who bragged about their long records, terrible exploits and severe sentences didn't get along much with Garino. He was known for being the head of a gang involved in small-time housebreaking and robbery of grocery stores and restaurants. It even seemed strange that they had sent him here. The veterans felt tarnished by such company.

"They send all kinds of shit here now," remarked 509, sentenced for three homicides.

"It's not like it used to be," commented another.

"What the hell! How come you came here for such a little thing?" Serpentina asked him one day.

Garino heard him and smiled, but did not respond.

Until one day Augusto asked him the same question. Now, to Garino, Augusto was not just anyone.

"I'm not here for the reason you think," he answered.

Then he told his story. In his parents' home, half the year was haunted by misery and hunger. In the hardest times, he and his siblings, as children, would resort to eating acorns, and many a day, acorns are what saved them. Acorns are not only good for pigs: Roasted acorns are actually delicious. During periods of unemployment the father participated in workers' protests or went out looking for some other job. One time, he was picked up and taken to Lisbon, where he was detained for some months. In the father's absences, the kids were forced to find whatever they could to eat. Garino didn't hesitate. He was not going to let his family die of hunger. He started by filching little things from stores and markets. Some fruit, potatoes, not much more. During that time only once did he dare reach out and grab a plucked chicken, but when he got home, his mother scolded him. She didn't beat him, only because he fled.

That was his first schooling. By the age of fourteen, figuring he wasn't getting anywhere that way, he joined up with two or three partners and decided to take on bigger things. Grocery stores and restaurants became well-known targets for their little gang's nighttime holdups. They wound up getting caught, tried in juvenile court, and sent to a reformatory, where they stayed almost two years.

"If you went to the reformatory, why did they sentence you here?" Augusto asked.

"I'll tell you later, I have to go now," said Garino walking away.

Late Night in Secret

Something weird happened one night on C Wing. Prisoners with insomnia were surprised by the extraordinary noises. Repeated crashing of the rotunda gates, hurried footsteps on cement, tramping up two flights of iron stairs, steps along the length of the second balcony, rattling locks and bolts, and then right away the same sounds in reverse direction until they could hear again the booming clank of the rotunda gates. Three times this series of noises repeated itself.

Parrana's cell was on the first balcony, exactly in front of the access stairway. When he heard the noise, he ran to look through the hatch whose cover was slightly raised. He saw indistinct figures passing by, three times coming and three times going.

The next day, no one knew where it started, but the news spread. Now it was clear why the evening before they had emptied the cells of C Wing's third balcony. The PIDE had brought three prisoners to the penitentiary, one by one. PIDE stood for Polícia Internacional e de Defesa do Estado, or International and State Defense Police, the feared and ruthless Portuguese security agency. People called one of their agents a Pide.

The three men were brought to their cells by a brigade, besides the prison's head guard and the head of the guards on the wing. The three were placed in cells separated by empty units, so they couldn't communicate by tapping on the walls. At one cell door, a Pide in mufti stood watch on a bench placed there for that purpose.

From then on, only Virgolino, a prisoner on special duty, and strictly watched by a Pide and by the guard of the wing, went around to the hatch in each of the three men's doors to bring and retrieve the necessities bucket and the mess tray. No one else could go up to the third balcony. Relieved every three hours, day and night, a Pide circled from end to end of the balcony from one side to the other, tirelessly spying through the peephole in each of the cells. And so it went for days, weeks and months.

From Short- to Long-Term Prison

To Silvino, everything plant or animal was sacred, so at recreation, he halted in his tracks at what he saw.

An enormous figure, Nero, was running around laughing and pulling a long string. At the end of it he had tied a rat he had somehow caught and was now dragging behind him. Looking backward, Nero kept his eyes on it to watch the effect. The animal no longer screeched or reacted. On its limp and bloody body only the little black dots of the eyes stood out.

Another prisoner couldn't contain himself: "Is this guy crazy or what?" And he started to stop him.

Gonçalo appeared in that precise moment. "Don't fuck with him, he'd just as soon kill you."

Oddly, Gonçalo was one of those people others really don't notice. Everyone knew who Nero was, as well as 509, Old Lady-Killer, Silvino, Augusto, 402, Tony, Serpentina, Catalan, and several others. If anyone were asked if he knew Gonçalo, no one would say yes. But this wasn't the first time it had happened: By who knows what coincidence he appeared, intervened speaking in his low, even voice, and in general, he was listened to. As he was this time.

There were reasons for his advice.

Nero had been apprehended half a dozen years before in his birthplace, the island of Madeira. A fight, a knifing, and a sentence of several months in prison. The sentence would have been left at that but for the fact that in the dungeon there a certain situation became aggravated.

Nero had cultivated the habit of mocking other people. And did he mock! Offensive, persistent, he didn't spare his mates from his crude jokes. That time, it turned out badly.

The other guy was a kindly simpleton who seemed like he would never harm anyone. Seated on his cot, he looked and listened and said nothing.

Nero started poking fun at him. "Hey, you weakling. You look like a wet noodle. Exactly. Like a wet noodle."

Wham-bang, he went at him all day. The fellow endured patiently, at first with a tolerant smile, then serious and annoyed.

"Hey, weakling," Nero redoubled his wisecracks. "Don't you hear? What's wrong with you, man? Don't you have a spoon to eat your noodles?" And laughing at his own jokes, he continued his routine.

At nightfall, the unforeseen happened. The disturbed simpleton rose in fury and shoved Nero. "Shut up, you son of a cuckold!"

Anything might have been expected, but not what happened.

Huge and imposing, Nero lifted the heavy workbench in the hall with Herculean might and hurled it at the guy's head, almost killing him.

Life-threatening assault, recidivism, court, trial, judgment: Nero went from short- to long-term prison and was transferred to the penitentiary.

His actions were a mixture of childishness and ferociousness. One day he could be lovingly caressing a cat that had wandered into the yard. The next day he was capable of chasing it away with a kick of his shoe. And worse. Men told how one time, to demonstrate his strength, he got hold of a cat by the back legs and ripped it apart from top to bottom.

At first glance, although heavy and huge, Nero looked like an okay fellow. But when crossed, his bursts of anger were terrifying.

Old Lady-Killer's Buried Money

They called him Old Lady-Killer, and he didn't mind. He seemed even proud to be called that. Many others were known by their numbers. Some, a few, by their real names. Still others by nicknames acquired either beforehand or by prison baptism. And others by their land or region of origin. Nicknames referring to the crime committed were rare. One of these was Old Lady-Killer.

Short, squeezed into his brown uniform, a man of blank looks and modest demeanor, no one noticed him in that Babylon of men marked by number. The only thing that stood out was his case. Not so much because he had killed, and not even for having killed an old lady—there were other similar cases. But because the whole penitentiary knew that his theft was considerable, and that while the author of the crime had been captured and sentenced, the haul had never been found. It was well hidden and secure out there, waiting for the end of his term.

Old Lady-Killer never spoke about it, but he appreciated others talking about it.

"So tell me, guy, how much did you get?" Garino asked him, half seriously and half joking, not so much to know but to make fun of him.

Old Lady-Killer kept his peace.

"Is it really in a safe place? Are you sure no one has discovered it?" Though serious, Serpentina chimed in out of curiosity.

No response. Old Lady-Killer didn't crack. His calm silence served him better than any explanations he might make.

The Christmas Visit

Christmas went as usual. Better meals, families bearing gifts. Everything meticulously inspected—ransacked, shaken, searched. Bread or cake cut into slices. Objects at times disassembled because wasn't there that time money was found tucked inside the head of a fried fish? And on another occasion, wasn't there a metal saw placed inside the sole of a shoe?

The atmosphere that day was festive and relaxed. Not for everyone, naturally. Augusto, Garino, Nero and Silvino, among others, never had visitors. For the dozens who had them it was a holiday.

Two prisoners stuck out for the large number of visitors they received: the Captain, a captain by profession and by name, sentenced for a series of frauds; and Viseu, an illiterate hemiplegic, sentenced for homicide.

As for the former, the number of visitors was not surprising. He enjoyed a certain protection, and it was whispered that some of those who visited him had other reasons apart from friendship. It was, in fact, peculiar. Aside from his wife, visitors that Christmas included a lawyer, an industrialist, and a high functionary. The artificial civility of the conversation could not cover up the obviously compromised nature of these relationships, explaining why these visits were even allowed. It was obviously not the Captain who had his debts to pay to the visitors.

As for Viseu, the crime of which he was accused had a mysterious history. According to what both guards and prisoners said, it was not clear why he had committed it, nor how he committed it, nor why he ran to the police in a rush to confess, which led to his sentencing.

"He can hardly move, and barely talk... He's a sad sack who has no idea what he's doing... Maybe he doesn't even know why he killed." Such were the things people commonly said.

To be or not to be capable of talking could be debated. But he said nothing to anyone.

It was truly a wonder how many visitors he received on Christmas what with the considerable expense for those trips and the overnights in the capital for an apparently poor family, the presents they brought, and the range of family members of all ages, including a healthy squad of youth and children. There was something quite exaggerated about it all.

Viseu seemed not to think it anything exceptional. Returning from his Christmas visit, lumbering awkwardly, his face shone with happiness.

For Nazaré, Christmas that year would change his whole life. Maybe because 31 inhabited a neighboring cell, it became customary to call them both at the same time to meet their visitors and place them in side-by-side visiting booths.

Along the stretch of a long counter, and under the vigilant watch of the guards, the prisoners were separated from their visitors by double panes of glass in which a circle of holes permitted voices to pass, though with difficulty. As everyone was shouting in order to be heard, it required not only attentiveness to the sound, but to the movement of lips and gestures, which served almost like a language for the deaf.

On that day, Nazaré couldn't concentrate his attention on his visiting mother. His glance wandered sideways to the face of a young woman visiting 31, a pretty face with enormous, moistly shining and caring eyes that lit up the semi-darkness of the visiting booth.

Rinaldo was the guard on duty that day, a booming bull of strength and barely repressed violence.

"Hey, you there!" he shouted threateningly to Nazaré. "Where are you looking?"

Nazaré pulled himself together. On the way back to their cells, he risked whispering to 31 by his side, "Is that your daughter?"

The enigmatic 31 did not respond right away.

"No," he said finally. "It's my sister."

"She's really something!" Nazaré couldn't refrain from saying.

The Vincentians

During recreation, after Sunday mass, civilians showed up to talk with a few inmates. These visitors always talked with the same few, because they were generally not well received. When one would pay them some attention, they would clutch at him like a barnacle and never let him go. They were the devotees of St. Vincent de Paul, patron saint of prisoners. Their generous mission was to bring help and comfort to the unfortunate. Help consisted of distributing an ounce of tobacco, moral comfort in catechism, and tame conversation.

Practicing his kindly mission for some years, Dr. Biscaia stood out, a pudgy little man with a sweet voice who never missed a single Sunday. Old Lady-Killer was one of his favorites. He'd discreetly place in his hands an ounce of tobacco, say a dozen or so words, and move on to someone else.

Old Lady-Killer took the tobacco eagerly and never even heard the doctor's words. And neither did he care to learn what Garino told him one day.

"Hey, buddy, you accept that crap? Do you know what that tobacco is? Do you know it's a mixture of rich men's cigarette butts? After a party, they collect the butts from the ashtrays, take them apart, and make those little packages they call ounces. Look carefully and you'll see burned tobacco they picked out by mistake."

Old Lady-Killer shrugged his shoulders.

"It's shameful," Garino added. "You're actually sucking on the saliva of those characters. You shouldn't accept it."

Old Lady-Killer nodded in agreement with Garino, but if he didn't smoke that, he had nothing else to smoke. So he accepted it.

Interrogations

The situation of the three political prisoners on C Wing's third balcony had gone unchanged for several months.

The prisoners knew of them but, accustomed to punishments and complicated conditions, spoke little about them. Besides which, they didn't appreciate political prisoners. Politicals, in the rare instances that they came here, were not obliged to wear the uniform and didn't have an identification number. One who had passed through, a well-known, influential personality, never spoke to anyone once he was granted recreation among the other prisoners, not even saying hello.

The three on C Wing were incommunicado, and up to then had not stirred any special interest or curiosity. What elicited the most comment was the fact that up there on the third balcony there was always a PIDE agent relieved every three hours. Everything seemed static and without incident—until one night there was news.

Virgolino, prisoner-on-duty for C Wing, was a light sleeper. One night, he awoke, startled by the violent crashing of the rotunda gate. Then, just like months before when the PIDE brought the three politicals, he heard quick footsteps, obviously of several people, echoing through the vast wing and, suddenly, treading up the metal staircase, the noisy opening of a cell on the balcony, and then once again noises of feet tracking in the opposite direction until the thundering clang of the gate and the silence that followed.

Later, as day was dawning, the same sounds repeated. A few nights later, yet again.

"They're taking one of those guys in for interrogation," Virgolino said to Parrana, whose cell on the second balcony was next to the circular staircase.

"Yes," Parrana agreed; he had also heard the noise. "I wouldn't want to be in his skin. They're sure doing a number on him now."

A few weeks passed, and the news spread that one of the prisoners on the C Wing third balcony had gone crazy and that PIDE had
removed him from the penitentiary. True or false, no one could say
for sure. But one thing was certain: From then on, Virgolino started
distributing the mess trays to only two cells on the third balcony.

Silvino, Insects and People

As a pulmonary tubercular, Silvino had crises that kept him in bed
for weeks on end. They just moved him to a cell in the infirmary, and
then he'd return to the wings.

Silvino was respected by all. A very particular form of respect—
not for having before him such a long sentence, which, sick as he
was, he likely wouldn't live to serve out. Nor for a long résumé of
robberies and break-ins. But because everyone—guards and prisoners alike—recognized him as a good man, a serious person, a man of
his word, and intelligent besides.

At times, he'd surprise people with his reflections on complex
problems. He didn't talk crap. He showed considered discernment.
No one could explain where such wisdom came from.

During recreation for the sick in the infirmary, when he could get
out of bed, and if time permitted, he'd circle around the rooftop garden. He looked distracted and self-absorbed. But he was observing
everything around him, which led, for example, to sensational dis-
coveries about insect life. He discovered spiders that cut stitches from
their own webs to free themselves of a bee, if by chance one had fallen
in; and they ran to attack and devour an intruder if it happened to be
a fly. He discovered that the African winged ant, with brown stripes
on its back, would flutter close to the ground until finding a fat caterpillar in the roots of a plant. It would then go some distance to find
a hiding place, come back and grab the caterpillar with unsuspected
force, happily dig a hole, inject its eggs into the caterpillar's body,
place the caterpillar in the hole, and cover and disguise the hole in an
artful work of construction worthy of a licensed engineer or architect.

If he appreciated animals that much, even more warmly did
he appreciate his companions. He treated everyone with esteem,
although without intimacy or superficial confidence because he didn't
engage in casual conversation, much less smutty talk. Speaking of
himself, he would say that while the life he led was a disaster, he
didn't deserve any other. In fact, he had never known either father or
mother. Trying to go back into his memory, the farthest he could reach
was seeing himself alone, maybe five or seven years old, begging in

the streets, reaching a furtive hand into the odd basket of fruit, and seeking shelter at night amidst market stalls or under some staircase. He knew, nonetheless, that with more intellect and willpower than he had, he could have followed a very different path in life.

Rolim's Show

The lack of a woman was for many the hardest punishment. They reacted in varying ways. They returned to their adolescence stimulating their own imagination and satisfying themselves. They sought out others for conversation, revelations and confessions. Those with greater resources paid dearly to Vianinha, master smuggler inside the prison, for photos of nude women. Many made detailed erotic plans for when they left prison. And many who entered desiring women grew over the years to desire men as well. Or were forced to accept them.

Amidst the abundance of talk on this topic, one group stood out which, with few variations in its makeup, gathered regularly during recreation in one corner of the enormous triangular yard. It was Rolim's show.

The group clustered to listen to him, because when it came to sex, Rolim was an ace. More than an ace, a maestro. Such extensive experience would be hard to explain.

The usual participants were almost all insignificant, timid people, men of ordinary crimes; at least they didn't discuss their past there. Given the subject, a naïve observer might find it strange that the prisoners sentenced for sex crimes showed complete disinterest in this little assemblage. None of them ever attended, nor even stopped within earshot to listen. Not Tony, who snatched the jewelry off the women he had raped, nor 101, who violated three of his own daughters, nor Elvas, who tied young women up to cork trees.

The only exception was Resmas, a decrepit dotard who, every time they allowed him to talk, bragged proudly about what he had done to a girl. Resmas was one of the first to join the group. And with a dirty smile and idiotic expression, he listened to everything from beginning to end without missing a word.

One day, Rolim asked one of the gathering how many women he had had sex with in his life, and the guy answered that, like all the other youth, he went to bordellos as a young man, then he married and, speaking honestly, from then on until he was arrested, he hadn't had any other woman.

"You're pitiful!" Rolim pronounced. "Prostitutes for sex are a false solution. And if you're talking about respectable women, there's not a single woman who has everything it takes to pleasure a man."

"Mine satisfied me," the man insisted.

"Then you'll spend your entire life never knowing what pleasure women can give you," Rolim scolded.

"You got that right," growled Serpentina, who had paused just outside the crowd and knew that the poor fellow still had many years ahead of him to serve. "Could be, he'll never have sex again anyway."

Another day, they were discussing feminine beauty.

"A woman is at her best at the age of thirty," said someone. "She still has the vitality of a girl but already the experience of a woman."

"For me," said another, "the younger, the tastier. There's nothing like busting a young girl's cherry. It's when they're the wildest and want to try it all."

Rolim already had his opinion.

"Breasts of 15, mouth of 20, thighs of 30, butt of 35, shoulders of 40, and sensual desire at every stage of life. Beauty is not only form," he explained. "A woman becomes different when she makes love. If she's passive and indifferent, then however beautiful she is, she's just an annoying tease. She could be so loud she's vulgar, a repulsive moron. But if she feels truthfully, breathes naturally, moans, even if she shouts, and in the end breaks into a smile with her eyes closed, showing pleasure that she doesn't want to let slip away, then that woman in that moment is a thousand times more beautiful than in any other moment of her life."

Rolim delivered his manifesto deliciously savoring his own eloquence.

While Rolim spoke, Argentino, a prisoner of uncommon bearing, approached the group. An Argentine, in fact, he gave the lie to the notion that South Americans are darker colored. Taller than most other prisoners, he was blond, with light skin and blue eyes. In his well-preserved fifty years, he walked among the others with apparent indifference. Calm and at ease, he stood near Rolim's group and listened blankly. It looked like he was paying attention, but no one could see what he was thinking about as Rolim was speaking.

Rolim continued talking, and Argentino removed himself as quietly as he had appeared.

Argentino Settling Accounts

Argentino's commanding posture distinguished him from the rest. He shared confidences with no one, and no one asked for it. This stance was curious though. His apparent isolation did not set him apart from the others. Despite something vague and slightly mysterious about him, they considered him one of their own.

Argentino was sentenced for having murdered a disloyal business associate while the man was sleeping, at close range, with a Colt. In a hail of 9-mm bullets, the last two aimed at his head—one in the temple, the other right between the eyes for good measure. There was talk of a "settling of accounts," but what kind of accounts no one knew.

The circumstances of the crime indicated a cold, considered, surgical mentality. That's how Argentino was known.

Augusto, 402, and 333 had also killed with a gun—in the heat of a skirmish or brawl, according to a certain social and moral code, or even legitimate self-defense. Not Argentino. The guy asleep, a rain of 9-mm from the Colt, followed by point blank shots in the temple and between the eyes. Maybe justified, but it was certainly performed like an execution.

The crime drew severe punishment, for in the eyes of the other prisoners, Argentino was known for having committed it. Later on, not by his own admission but owing to indiscretion by the guards, the rest of his past become better known, though not all of it. In the light of this history, his coldblooded execution of a business partner who betrayed him seemed like only one fateful moment in a much longer series of other, perhaps even more serious, crimes.

Falua Opens a Padlock

The same, monotonous everyday life over the passage of years was interrupted by a few episodes that went down in history—such as the event that happened with Falua one day.

Falua didn't like talking about his exploits. As far as anyone knows, only three times did he ever reveal his expertise in crime. If he didn't convince you, at least he put on a good act.

One time, the specialists were discussing the best way to break into a door without making noise. Falua answered the others with haughty confidence.

"No crowbar, no lever," he said in his high-pitched voice. "Insert a soaking wet wedge of wood under the door and go take a walk. Go sit in a café or go whoring, you'll have time. When you come back, the door will be open."

Another time, they were arguing about breaking into a church door. False keys and shattering the lock came up. Someone even remembered the soaking wet wedge.

"Don't even think about it," Falua pronounced. "Church doors weigh a ton. By that method, you'd be waiting your whole life. There's only one way. Bore a hole through the door, stick a sharp saw through it and cut the wood all around the lock. It will come out whole, and you stick your arm in and open the door from the inside."

Some believed him, others not. Those most familiar with such business called him a lying impostor. But that day he showed them all up.

At recreation, Clemente was the usual guard on duty. In his relations with the prisoners, he frequently erupted in bursts of brusque aggression. At the same time, he was quite familiar with them and enjoyed testing them.

"You guys think you can do anything," said Clemente, "but you're just braggarts. Look at the padlock on that gate. Not one of you is capable of opening it"—and he looked around triumphantly, sure that none would accept his challenge.

"Can I try?" It was the high voice of Falua, his foxy eyes smiling.

The guard refused at first, then hesitated. Falua insisted, and the guard, turning to see if any of his colleagues might be watching, wound up authorizing this demonstration of skill.

Taking care that Falua didn't see, the guard spun the combination lock with its six cylinders of ten numerals. The heavy lock was clamped onto a thick chain threaded through the two halves of the gate. With the lock closed and the combination scrambled, the guard leaned back and waited.

Falua requested several meters of string. He separated it into strips and passed each strip through each one of the lock's six cylinders. For each cylinder, he told one of his fellow prisoners to simultaneously grasp both ends of the piece of string and rapidly, energetically cause the discs to roll from back to front.

The operation commenced. Falua's assistants stationed themselves around the lock and worked the strings hard, back and forth. It took a while. The audience grew, and the guard started laughing.

"Go for it, Falua!" he mocked. "At this rate, you'll wind up opening the gates of hell!"

Everyone chuckled heartily, when suddenly a sharp snap rang out and the lock fell open.

That story got repeated from generation to generation. Falua was no longer simply Falua. He became recognized and renamed as The Guy Who Opened the Padlock of the Gate with a String.

402 Tries and Fails

402 wasn't lying when he told Augusto that one day, if he wanted to speak with him, he would no longer be here. This was his solid plan. Since he had been sentenced and brought here, he had thought of nothing else. A seaman practically since childhood, he had strength, agility and courage enough to pursue any scheme. He wasn't inclined toward complicated plans. His willpower and the urgency he felt to see himself on the outside led him to concentrate his attention on possibilities for the shortest, simplest and fastest way out.

For the first four years, on the rare occasions when he moved about the prison, he carefully noted where he was closest to the street. He would calculate the obstacles one by one. And he sketched out a plan. He'd be on the list of prisoners going to the infirmary; then at a specific spot, he'd evade the guard's watch, linger behind a few seconds on the march, climb up a conduit to the roof of the canteen storeroom, try to run and keep from being seen by the first sentinel, creep along the roof, hop onto the building that faced onto the street, get to the battlement of white stone on the wall, and go for broke. Even within view of a second sentinel, he'd jump and run away down the street.

That's how he imagined it, and that's what he did. Up to the wall, easier and faster than he anticipated. Upon reaching the battlement, he felt dazzled by the long street with lots of people and vehicles that ran along the front of the building in bright sun. And then the surprise: The cobbled sidewalk was way, way down. The height of the wall was much greater than he had figured. He hesitated a second. Freedom, however, was there within reach. He jumped into space.

The gunshot from a guard didn't hit him. What he thought was the easiest part is what failed at the last moment. Falling heavily on the stone walkway, he couldn't get up. Pinned to the ground by a broken, bloody leg, there he sat, to the shock of the passersby, until the flustered guards came running out to bring him back inside. His bad luck, in that group of guards came Rinaldo and Bazuca, who both enjoyed beating prisoners. Despite the fact that he was wounded, they dragged him away, punching and kicking him without cease.

His fractured, poorly treated tibia gave way to a permanently infected, deep, ulcerated wound. The moment at which the man of high hopes had attempted to restart his life turned into the beginning of a slow, inexorable agony.

A Fatal Hunger Strike

The case of the Communist prisoners on the C Wing third balcony suddenly got intense. For several days now, one of the remaining two refused to eat. Going to fetch his meal trays, Virgolino found them just as he had left them.

Accompanied by the Pide on duty and the guard on the wing, the infirmary chief visited the cell with the lead guard. In front of the Pide, both of them pretended that they saw nothing unusual. The prisoner was conducting a hunger strike, but no measures were taken.

News spread throughout the prison, reaching Garino, and from him to Augusto the gardener.

"PIDE couldn't care less," said Augusto. "On the outside no one has any knowledge of it. If the guy takes this thing any further, as far as they're concerned, they'll let him die and say it was an illness."

A month later, Augusto met Garino. "Do you know anything?" he asked.

"I saw Virgolino. The man keeps not eating, and he's on the verge of passing away."

Garino was right. A few days later, at quiet time, they went to get him from his cell and removed him on a stretcher to the infirmary. The guard chief, other guards, two Pides, Benjamim and other infirmary staff called upon for the transport, filled the infirmary cell and stayed packed in there. The doctor and the nurse came in response to the crisis. Skeletal, his flesh an earth color, jaw and teeth outlined under his skin, his sunken eyes closed, the man presented no sign of life. The doctor felt his neck, tried to open his eyelids, took his pulse and, opening his shirt, exposed a shaggy trunk just skin and bones.

"How many days has he been like this?" the doctor asked.

They told him several days already.

At that moment, the Pides noticed that, in the excitement of the event, all those people had witnessed the scene.

"Out of here! Everyone out," they shouted loudly, sending everyone elbowing one another out.

Benjamim weighed more than 100 kilos and had tremendous power. He observed all this indignantly. A crazy desire to shout out came into his head, to accuse them, to kick them out, to pummel them with his fists. But it passed. He left with the others.

From then on, few had any idea what happened. But for sure, the man was dead.

"The guy was firm," Silvino commented, "but he died. Was it worth it?"

"He didn't die," Garino corrected. "They killed him."

Nazaré's Courtship Begins

Over the course of two years, Nazaré's and 31's side-by-side visits occurred three or four times. Nazaré anticipated these visits anxiously. Not on account of his mother or the gifts she brought him, but because he could see and gape at 31's sister for more than half an hour. Although it occurred only very occasionally, that visit became, for Nazaré, the most important event of his life in prison.

Returning to their cells, or during recreation time, Nazaré kept talking about her. 31 was a man of few words. With his immovable face, it was hard to guess what he was thinking. But after two years, and many snippets of conversation, Nazaré reached some clarity.

"I really like her," Nazaré told him confidentially, and with a sense of relief, awaited his reaction.

31 turned to face him and paused a beat. He didn't seem to hesitate. The words came out naturally and honestly as if confirming a long-known truth.

"She likes you too. Just today she told me so again."

That night Nazaré hardly slept. He couldn't get the girl's face, or her look, out of his head. He imagined a dazzling future. In his mind, he rehearsed every word of his next conversation with 31. He could not lose this breath of luck. He had to move things forward.

So, three days later during recreation, with his talk all set, his speech came out whole and faultless.

"Hey, 31. Listen to what I want to tell you. I truly like your sister. I'm 25 years old and I have five years to go on my sentence. You told me she likes me, too. For my part, I'm really serious. Couldn't I write to her?"

31 stopped, turned around and looked at him straight in the eyes, silent, reserved and undecipherable. His words, as always, were plain and simple.

"I've thought about that too, bud. It's good you spoke up. I'm not leaving here for another eight years and she needs someone to support her. And you'll be out in five. I'll give you her address. The rest is up to you."

A few weeks later, 31 gave Nazaré her address. And that's how a love story began.

An Attack No One Saw

In a far corner of C Wing's recreation area, a little commotion stirred up. It happened quickly. To some, it seemed like the beginning of a fight. Then everything reverted to quiet and normal. Only later they noticed one of the prisoners buckled on the ground, half leaning against the workshop wall, with his face all bloody.

The others proceeded with their recreation as if they'd seen nothing. Even Silvino, always so observant, passed right by as though he hadn't noticed. Only after quite some time did a guard come by and see the fallen man. He fired off a salvo of questions. What happened? Who was it? Why? No one knew anything. Or if they knew, they didn't say. Not even the one with the lesions.

At the end of recreation, they lined up and returned to their cells. On the way, Serpentina said to the fellow by his side, "It was 509."

"Did you see him?"

"Yeah."

He did, in fact, see him. He didn't witness the reason for the conflict, but 509 came up quickly and powerfully, grabbed the other guy by the shoulders and, using his head, smashed him right in the face.

"I wanted to ..." muttered an anguished Serpentina.

"What could you have done?" the fellow consoled him.

You can be sure no one ratted on 509. The risk would have been too high.

His figure rose above the rest. Not that 509 was a showoff. But besides his size, people saw in his cocky carriage a brute force ready to be unchained. They particularly saw his bowed legs, his head firmly braced on his stiff neck and a tight, compact expression with his tiny eyes fixed into the distance.

"That's it," one prisoner observed, "Wild Boar creates fear—"

"Shut up, stupid," another companion interrupted. "Don't even whisper that name. If he hears you, you're toast."

Indeed, no one dared utter that name. For such carelessness, several had already paid dearly. In truth, 509 did inspire fear. He had already been there a number of years and still had fifteen more to go. The list of brutalities attributed to him was extremely long.

Death in the Cardboard Workshop

It happened in the cardboard workshop. Nero had not lost his amusement at throwing insults at his fellow prisoners. The more afraid of him others felt, the more offensive and humiliating his taunts. There were good reasons to fear him: his massiveness and his reputation. That day, he directed his hatefulness toward some insignificant type that no one paid attention to.

"Hey, fatty," Nero fired at him with a guffaw. "How come you stick your ass out when you're cutting cardboard? Huh? How come?"

Just as it happened in the dungeon back in Madeira, *bim-bam*, all morning long he attacked the guy. The little man didn't react at all—neither a little nor a lot. The guard on duty even found it funny. But another prisoner observed this scene play out with manifest unhappiness. He was offended by Nero's evermore gross and nasty provocations, as well as by the other guy continuing his work as though he heard nothing. Finally, he couldn't hold back, and murmured, "If that was me ..."

Nero looked at him sideways with disgust and continued merrily shooting off his mouth.

"Hey, fatso. Damn, you look like a girl from the slums puttin' your butt out like that—"

Once again, the other prisoner said under his breath, "If he said that to me, I wouldn't be ..."

He said it only to himself in a barely audible voice. The trouble is, Nero heard him.

No one would ever forget what happened. Nero took two quick steps, drawing his voluminous body toward the other prisoner. Fuming with rage and letting out a howl, he buried his work knife into his fellow prisoner's chest, pushing the blade in with all his body weight.

The guards came running, the victim was taken away, and Nero was immediately brought to a penalty cell in the basement. He would be locked up there for more than three months.

Crime Weapons

By the mysterious process of communication throughout the over-all system of separation and isolation in the wings, the death in the cardboard workshop quickly became known all around the prison. For two or three days, at recreation and in the brief words exchanged in casual encounters, it was the primary topic.

The word "homicide" classifies the crime, but neither describes nor characterizes it. Different situations, different reasons, different motivations, different weapons.

Commenting on the cardboard workshop death, everyone focused on a single aspect of the incident. The mistake on the prison admin-istration's part was to allow Nero to work in that shop after having nearly killed someone in the Madeira dungeon. Questionable per-missiveness as to the provocative insults. The responsibility of the dead guy for interfering where he shouldn't have. The lack of super-vision by the guard on duty. About each one of these facets there were various opinions; people would argue over them for years.

Also, about the work knife, the crime weapon.

In the end, anything can be used to kill. Revolver and pistol. A hunting rifle and a closed-barrel shotgun. Switchblade, knife and dagger. Ax, hoe and iron bar. Stones and rocks. Ropes and belts. An infinite variety of poisons. Also, bare arms that strangle and destroy. A thousand and one ways of killing.

At recreation, in the sun, a group weighed the subject. Some expanded the conversation to analyze the complex strategies of well-known cases.

"What are you jerks talking about?" demanded a young man with a weak voice, a usually bashful and quiet guy. "I stabbed a guy with an umbrella. It went into his gut like a bayonet."

The others laughed, and the scoffing would have continued if one of the others present, a man with a shrewd face and a flutey, mocking voice, hadn't added a novel and surprising element to consider.

"You laugh? An umbrella is a heavy weapon. It's nothing special. A well-sharpened pencil used correctly does the same job."

Once again, everybody laughed. Only one man present thought it too much to joke about such grave things.

"Be serious, boy. This stuff is for men."

"Taking a guy out with a gunshot takes no skill," replied the shrewd-faced guy, who knew that the opponent in his case was armed with a pistol. "With a pencil, you can show how good you are."

Tempers heated up, the guards took note and approached, and the group melted.

"The man is an idiot with his stories," someone remarked stepping away.

"Stories?" another corrected. "He cleaned the guts out of a guy with a well-sharpened pencil. Sounds impossible, but that's what he did."

Working for Social Re-Entry

The death in the cardboard workshop served as a pretext for endless talk about the workshops. There were three: the cardboard one, another assembling motorbikes, and furniture, all private businesses that cleared super-profits thanks to the miserable wages. Set up in the barracks that circled around the enormous compound comprised of the wings in the star, the workshops were extolled by the Ministry of Justice, Prison Services, and the prison administration as the sure path (according to them) toward the delinquents' "repair" and "social rehabilitation." First, the habit of working and receiving recompense would by itself remove the temptation toward crime. And second, it would offer the prisoners the potential to gather a goodly sum in a Reserve Fund so that when they exited into freedom, they would have enough money for their re-entry into society. The prisoners' own opinions, however, did not align with such notions.

For several weeks after what occurred, no one spoke of anything else in the cardboard workshop.

"Those who sent Nero here," said one, "are the ones responsible. They should have known that sooner or later something like this would happen."

Others used the occasion to give voice to their discontentment, worries and anxieties.

"I'm fed up," said another. "I've been here five years cutting cardboard for packaging and I still have ten years of my sentence to go. I can't bear this. Spending another ten years cutting cardboard to earn a few pennies? And if the business ends before that? It's a swindle, that's all it is."

Porto Alto had clearer ideas. Coming from Benavente, he spoke about bulls and bullfights as though he had never done anything else in his life. Still, he always revealed himself to be a man of much broader knowledge and experience. He had labored two or three years in the workshops. Then he refused to continue there, and he explained why.

"What they give us is miserable. And from that misery they take almost everything from us. We pay for the cell, we pay for the meals, we pay for the use and washing of clothes, we pay for everything as if we were in a hotel. Two thirds of what they give us they take away. Up to now, the Access Fund gave me only enough for tobacco and paper and stamps to write to my family. And the Reserve Fund? How much would they hand me when I leave ten years from now? Fifteen years from now? And how long would it last? Two or three days?"

People talked outside the workshops, too. 333, vested as a sacristan at Sunday mass and in other important responsibilities, had a less materialist view. First, he presented some numbers. In internal work inside the prison, there were fewer than fifty prisoners. Four aides per wing, plus half a dozen cleaning people in the rest of the facility, plus four or five in the gardens, and a few more in odd work, such as loading, the library, the chapel and sacristy.

"So, you can see," 333 explained, "at most a hundred who work. And the other four hundred?"

But he didn't limit himself to posing the question. Talking to the priest on Sunday, or when he got the chance with the guards, and even with the head guard, he refined his conclusion. Yes, work was important, but that's not what decided the future.

"Those of us who sinned can only find salvation in repentance before God and in the hope for His mercy."

"That guy truly believes," said the head guard.

"A fraud, that's what he is," said Ernesto the guard.

Garino's Most Serious Crime

Garino had promised Augusto that he'd recount the rest of his story. It took a while, several months, because they didn't find each other either at work or at recreation. At the first opportunity, he fulfilled his promise.

Yes, it was something more serious. It happened during one of the long periods of unemployment and hunger that swept through the big Alentejo estates. The workers demonstrated, went to the city council to demand work and protested against the government. The only response they got was getting charged by the National Republican Guard, the prompt arrival of brigades from the PIDE, beatings and jails. Unemployment stayed the same; the black hunger, also the same.

That's when Garino played a game with higher stakes. With two or three of his young friends from his former group that raided grocery stores, he devised an audacious plan. First, they went by night to a rich man's stable and "borrowed" a couple of healthy mules that they saddled up the best they could. Then they went to a farm, which they had cased out as a supply storehouse. Once they broke through the door, they had only to load up and haul off. A few sacks of wheat, others of potatoes and beans, and whatever they found in a salting barn. Then they rode around to villages and houses distributing the wealth.

Discovered and caught, they appeared before the court. Charged with breaking and entering, robbery and criminal organization, they were all sentenced. As the recognized and self-confessed chief of the operation, Garino earned the biggest portion: twelve years in prison.

Before handing down the sentence, the judge looked at the accused with a fixed gaze: "You can't complain about the sentence. Actually, I was generous. You're a Communist, that's what you are!" he said implacably.

"Meee? A Communist?" Garino exclaimed, genuinely shocked.

Now he could laugh at the scene, for since then he had learned quite a bit. "I guess I was, but I didn't know it at the time," he told Augusto as he ironically concluded his story.

"They gave it to you hard," Augusto commented.

"Nah," said Garino, "it was one of the most sensible things I ever did in my life."

A Fortune of 300 Contos Waiting

If there was any doubt concerning what Old Lady-Killer had stolen, he himself one day dispelled it. It was Serpentina who got it out of him. When he wanted to yank the truth out of someone, Serpentina didn't ask questions. He would bombard them with affirmations, with insinuations, suppositions, slurs and insults, and surround and confuse in such a way that the victim wound up letting some hidden truth escape.

So it was that day. Serpentina pestered and annoyed him so much that after bearing it silently and passively, Old Lady-Killer exploded. "You think three hundred *contos* isn't much? Add it up. Would I ever earn that much in a lifetime? I've only got three more years here. After that, I'll be living okay."

Serpentina expected anything, but three hundred *contos* were astounding. That was enough to buy a nice house. He was amazed.

The minute he had spoken, Old Lady-Killer regretted it.

"I only told this to you. Now don't be going around telling anyone—"

"What do you take me for?" Serpentina retorted. "I heard nothing, I know nothing. It's like you were talking to a priest."

There's no proof it was Serpentina who spread the news. But surely in time the whole prison knew about it. It was a shock.

"That guy you see there," Bazuca told a new guard at the penitentiary, "no one pays him any mind. He killed an old lady and now he has three hundred *contos* that he stole stashed away real well. Nobody even notices him, but he's one smart cookie."

An Appeal for Help

Virgolino woke up in the middle of the night with the impression that he had heard the sound of a switch being pulled, and then the respective alarm echoed through the fog of silence in the vast space of the wing. He waited a moment to hear the strong metallic sound, from the central tower, of a gate opening for a guard to pass to see what the matter was. He heard nothing. A few minutes later, the sound of the switch repeated, and unexpectedly, one after another, the peal of the alarm. Someone was in trouble. There was no reaction from the central tower, and again everything fell into silence, interrupted for a few seconds only by a cavernous coughing coming from someplace. Time passed, and Virgolino went back to sleep.

Early in the morning, before dawn even, Rinaldo and another guard opened his cell door.

"Get out!" they ordered.

With hurried strides, they took him to the end of the first balcony. Another guard was standing next to the open door of a cell. Inside, his body half on the bed and half off, lay a prisoner—dead.

"We have to get him out of here before the next shift," Rinaldo said. "You and Benjamim from the infirmary will do the job."

Virgolino recalled what he had heard in the night.

"Last night I heard—"

"What did you hear, say it!" Rinaldo violently interrupted.

"—the alarm sounded three times, I heard—"

"You didn't hear nothing, is that clear?"

For a moment, Virgolino looked at the guard, imposing, stiff, threatening, triggered for brutal aggression. Virgolino saw they wanted to cover up any blame. What could he do? He hesitated—and complied.

Nero Leaves Isolation in a Rage

Nero was taken out of isolation that day. He had spent several months in darkness. He howled against his punishment. He refused to eat for almost a week. Eventually, he calmed down. Either he'd walk his bodily bulk back and forth, hour after hour, in the small dark cell, or he'd lie down on his cot for days on end sleeping or dozing. Sometimes he'd be yelling with all his lung power, but from the subterranean depths only vague, undecipherable sounds could be heard through the immensity of the wings.

"Let's go, it's over," said the guard Clemente, opening the isolation cell door late one afternoon. "Grab your blanket and cup and come out."

Nero stretched and cracked his limbs, yawned loudly, eyes squinted on leaving the darkness, said nothing and followed the guards. On the way, they tried to engage him in conversation without effect. They led him to a cell in one of the wings and left.

It wasn't long before a tremendous uproar arose. The guard on duty ran to look through the peephole, and what he saw appalled him. He couldn't believe what he was seeing.

Nero looked like a madman. He'd broken the bench into pieces, demolished the poor bed and removed parts of its metal frame, and with those rods he destroyed the metal basin and shattered the glass in the door hatch. The mattress, made of rye straw, was ripped open, and the straw, floating in the air with fragments of iron and wood, rose up in a tornado of hurtled blows. Nero howled, spun and gesticulated as if he were on a battlefield.

More guards arrived, but they didn't dare open the door and put an end to the madness. Only hours later did Nero let up. Suddenly relaxing, he collapsed onto the rubble and fell asleep.

The guards looked in on him, met and decided to leave him there until the next day. In the morning, Nero awoke, bewildered, stretched his arms raising and twisting them, looked around and, with surprise, surveyed what he had done. He looked two or three times. Then he raised his hands to his head and started laughing wildly.

"Ay, Holy Mother of God!" he shouted and laughed. "Ay, Our Lady my love!"

A guard looked in and shrugged his shoulders. After the lineup and count-off, after the distribution of mugs of coffee and bread crusts, three guards opened his door and escorted him to another cell. The laughing had stopped. Silent and at peace, he allowed himself to be led away.

Crime and Man

Whoever saw them, in their lineups, their movements, at recreation, in that chestnut blur of uniforms stamped in white with big identification numbers and noisily shuffling their clogs and slippers, would tend to see all those men pretty much alike, one to another, not just in the way they looked, but for the evil they had committed. But such a view would be highly mistaken.

Every condemned man could be classified in judicial terms according to the crime committed: homicide, assault, fraud, theft, rape. But solely by the crime committed, no rigorous classification can be made of them as human beings. Classified in legal terms alone, the crime does not in and of itself define the man.

Hundreds of prisoners were sentenced for homicide. All had killed. Still, the act itself, its determinants, its environment, circumstances and execution, and at times, their behavior after the fact, were so diverse as to also show their human differences. Cases ranged from ferocity bordering on horror and madness to others reflecting civic righteousness and even moral courage.

Augusto, for example, had been moved to indignation over the most horrible felonies that a big landowner had committed against his own family—seduction and abandonment of a sister, and expulsion from land and home after a long series of harassments. Augusto killed the man with one shot of a shotgun, with the aggravating factor of premeditation.

402, as a sailor, killed someone in a fight one night on the Cais do Sodré. It was legitimate self-defense, but he didn't invoke that at the trial. Besides, his feelings, ideas and attitudes were positive and generous.

There were also all kind of thieves and robbers. Cases of malevolence, violence and cruelty, instances of decent men propelled into action by society and personal life circumstances. Like Garino, or like Silvino.

Also, with respect to those sentenced for rape, you can't judge everyone simply under the judicial classification of the crime.

Tony assaulted women on deserted roads, dragged them to the gutter, raping them as he tore off their earrings, lacerating their earlobes with a brutal yank. Elvas the smuggler tied girls up to cork trees and left them there afterward. 101 abused his power as a father and raped his three daughters. 325 intimidated his victims with a sharp knife to their throats. The four from Leiria had kidnapped and gang-raped a girl, leaving her naked, black and blue, and half crazed in a deserted pine forest. No one quite knew what Resmas, the decrepit old man, did, but with a dumb smile, he would brag about his deed like the biggest event of his life.

Surely, 230 could not be judged in the same way. He was sentenced for raping a girl of twelve in the house where he lived. Prematurely developed, this lively child-woman with a beautiful, shapely body came on to him, exhibiting herself, provoking and challenging him. One time she ran to his room when he had already gone to bed and kissed him, leaving behind the fleeting image of her nakedness and excitement. 230 couldn't resist any longer. He went to her, she refused him, he forced her without any forethought of doing so, the girl shouted, the family woke up, and it wound up with the police and court. At the trial, 230 did not cite all that preceded his act. The rape of a child was proved, and 230 received a heavy sentence— heavier than Tony or the four from Leiria got.

To know each man there, it's not enough to say he killed, robbed, assaulted, defrauded or raped. It's been said that there aren't crimes, just criminals. Many who committed crimes could well have spent their whole lives without doing them.

The Prisoner in Isolation on the Third Balcony

The rule was separation of the prisoners on the six wings. Ordered by the guards' whistles, brought out of their cells in formation, the prisoners of each wing were led in turn for one hour a day into the open air in the large triangular spaces that divided the immense walls of the building. Above all, it was there that people got to know one another. There were no dining rooms where the prisoners could see each other: Food plates came from the kitchen on trays and were distributed to each cell. So it was that, except for moving from one wing to another on duty, each prisoner—for five, ten, twenty or more years that they spent there—ended up directly knowing only a limited number of the others. Or met someone and then didn't see them for many years. Opportunities to meet prisoners from different wings happened only at mass, at the medical office and in the infirmary recreation time, since sick men from all the wings went to the infirmary, always under strict observation.

Augusto the gardener, whose cell was in A Wing, hadn't met anyone from C Wing for a long time. It was only by chance that he met Parrana from C Wing at the infirmary's treatment center. They were in line one behind the other.

"So?" Augusto risked saying in a whisper. "The political is still there?"

Parrana made sure the guards weren't listening. "There's only one. Another went crazy, and the other they killed. There's just one."

"Still in isolation?"

"Yes," Parrana responded. "Only Virgolino can take his meals to him. They don't allow anyone else to go there. Aside from Virgolino, no one else has even seen his face."

Augusto shook his head. "It's too much. It's more than two years they've had him locked up like that. Really too much."

"More than three years," Parrana corrected.

The guard approached and the nurse called out, irritated. "Hey, you! Are you here for treatment or to shoot the breeze? It's your turn, get over here."

333 Defending His Honor

333 was likely the prisoner who most enjoyed the confidence of the director, the head guard, the priest, the doctor, the nurse and the cook. Some of the best jobs assigned to prisoners went to him. He was the sacristan at Sunday mass, the person responsible at the library for distributing and collecting books, however few there were, and for delivering milk to the seriously ill, which wasn't that often but was still a critical responsibility.

Courtly toward everyone, he bowed left and right. His skinny features looked like they were carved by a knife, his sunken eyes shining and eager. The austerity of his features was offset, however, by friendly gestures, a gentle voice, thoughtful language and smooth talking that he used with everyone. He addressed the director as Your Excellency Mister Director, the head of the guards as Mister Chief Guard, the lower-level guards as Mister followed by their names which he knew by heart. He treated the other prisoners as brothers or friends, distinguishing them, though, according to their social origin: He called a doctor Doctor, a captain Captain, an engineer Engineer and so forth. Toward the most humble, he spoke from on high with a protective air. Some enjoyed such mannerisms, while others said it was 333 who enjoyed himself at their expense.

333's case had been famous. Three men had a commercial partnership. Business was going badly, and money wasn't coming in. The way he himself frankly put it, he had only one alternative: Either grab something for his own security before the business went belly-up or go into debt to the others. Nothing wrong with a man choosing to survive. Instead of paying the bills, he just put the dough in his pocket.

All natural and logical, as anyone could see, and as he said. However, the others disagreed. They forced an encounter, showing him their papers and, reviewing the numbers, called him a thief. Up to that point, things hadn't gone so badly, but the accusation ruined everything. Tempers rose, they shouted, started fighting and, to put an end to the nonsense, 333 pulled out a pistol and *bam! bam!* killed his partners on the spot.

As always, Garino commented, "This story sounds made up, but that's exactly what happened."

In fact, as 333 said, how could it have gone any other way?

"Your Honor will understand, I couldn't do anything else," he explained in court. "It was in defense of my honor."

Absurd though it may appear, it seems the judge understood the defendant so well that his sentence was relatively light.

Now some years had passed, but 333 worked out a strategy: Employing his unique style, he was fighting for conditional release.

The Badass Malveira

Some of the guards enjoyed putting to the test those prisoners who arrived with the reputation of a bully. They directed jokes at them, offended, annoyed and threatened them. If the prisoner reacted in any way, he'd get punished in proportion.

Nero and 509 (Wild Boar) had been subjected to the test. The facts demonstrated that in those cases, there were only two responses from the authorities: Either close your eyes, or face brutal violence leading to deaths sooner or later. The authorities chose to close their eyes.

Malveira was no exception to the rule. He entered the penitentiary with the reputation of a badass and was subjected to the test. He sported a rap sheet of snarly cattle deals, fights, a homicide, and pulled a heavy sentence. He wasn't tall or strong. Angular and bony, his whole being broke up into brusque movements as if stiffened by a powerful internal pressure.

The guards started to experiment with him.

"Hey, Malveira! Clean up that water from the floor for me."

Malveira gave that guard a dirty look, but he cleaned.

"Not clean enough, clean better!"

Malveira repeated cleaning what was already clean.

"Are you blind or what?! Don't act so refined. Clean it with some elbow grease."

That was the last straw. Malveira huffed and threw the mop. "You know what, Mister Guard? Go to hell!"

That was how the first test ended. That phrase cost him a week in solitary with bread and water. And the guards didn't refrain from goading him further.

"This one is no Nero, and not even a Wild Boar," remarked Bazuca, wanting for opportunities to rake him over the coals. "He wants to be a hardass, but the hot air's gonna empty out fast."

"We'll see," Clemente answered. "The guy is small, but he seems bold. He'll make us work."

The provocations continued.

"Hey, Malveira!" Bazuca shot at him one day. "One more time, wash that mess kit better."

"Hey, Malveira! Over there!" he shot at him again. "Quiet in line, don't be a sissy, ya hear?"

Malveira gave outward signs of docility. He didn't react to the taunts, but any attentive observer could see that the tension he hoarded would inevitably break out one day in a fury.

Doctor Barnabé: Thish Will Pash

The old doctor wasn't such a bad fellow. He couldn't do great things, but did what he could. He received the sick and those who complained of being sick, dispensed the few medicines he had at his disposal, kept the most serious cases in the infirmary cells and reserved the rest of the cells for short-term patients.

When the state of the Communist on the third balcony of Wing C who went on a hunger strike became aggravated, the Pides who by turns stood permanent guard outside his cell never called the doctor or nurse. They transported his failing body to an infirmary cell, where he died shortly after. They wanted to force the doctor to sign a death certificate, but he refused and ordered an autopsy.

"Not everyone would be that courageous," said Benjamim, when he spoke of it to Augusto the gardener.

One day, however, that doctor left, and they sent another. No one knew where the old one went nor where the new one came from. To be sure, the new one was hardly young in age. To the contrary, he was rather up in years, deaf as a doorpost and completely senile. No one knew his real name. But someone gave him one, and from then on, he was forever known as Doctor Barnabé.

402 attributed to him the worsening of the big lesion on his leg that resulted from his fall when he tried to escape. At first, when the old doctor was still around, they treated the wound. Barnabé came and did nothing for him for a long time.

Finally, they brought him to the office. The nurse removed the enormous bloody dressing and Barnabé gave a quick look.

"Thish will pash," he said solemnly in his extreme regional accent.

From all appearances, this was Barnabé's preferred expression whenever he saw a patient.

Porto Alto was diabetic in a markedly advanced stage of his illness. Resources were few, but the nurse, in a good mood that day, remembered there were still a few ampules of insulin, and he shouted into the doctor's ear that he should give one to the sick man.

"Inshu what?" Doctor Barnabé asked.

The nurse gave Porto Alto the injection, and when he was ready to return to his cell on the wing, the doctor wanted to console him.

"Thish will pash," he said paternalistically.

But it didn't pass. They found him; he had fainted in his cell. Benjamim and one other were called to carry him to the infirmary.

"Hypoglycemia," the nurse shouted into Barnabé's ear.

"Hypo what?" the doctor seemed surprised.

Benjamim was an infirmary aide for several years. He had already seen similar cases. He ran to his own cell to fetch a little sugar, placed the sugar in Porto Alto's mouth, and in a few moments, he became himself again.

The nurse did nothing more and didn't intend to do anything more, so he didn't intervene. Benjamim was known as peaceable and disciplined. He performed his work as an aide and other, even less agreeable tasks, such as transporting suicides and other corpses. He was always available for whatever was needed. He weighed more than a hundred kilos, and the nurse knew it was better not to arouse bad feelings by crossing him.

Is the Maestro a Charlatan?

Rolim's group never failed. The usual participants listened to him with wonderment at his wisdom. When doubts, new problems or disagreements arose, Rolim found just the right response and comfortably dominated the conversation.

His lectures about the importance, for the true pleasure of the man, to know how to give pleasure to the woman, continued meanwhile to raise questions and even discord.

"If the woman is frigid, my friend, there's nothing to be done," one of his listeners piped up that day.

"You're mistaken," replied Rolim. "She's frigid only because you don't know how to guide her."

"Forget it," his listener said. "If she's frigid, how you gonna guide her?"

"When I was a young man," Rolim expounded, "all I wanted was to jump on top of them. It hardly left any time for anything. I just wanted to cum."

"And then?"

"Then, if I went on acting like that, I would never have truly known a woman. You can only reach your greatest pleasure when you also give the greatest pleasure to your partner."

"That's what I did," bragged another participant in the conversation. "They couldn't complain. I'd stick it to them two or three times in a row."

"What's wrong with you?" another cut him off. "I'd fuck five or six times."

"Me, I'd do it ten or twenty times," Serpentina mocked.

"That's not the issue," Rolim smiled condescendingly. "One time could be better than many. The important thing is to prepare the woman. Hold back, discover her most sensitive points—many times in places you wouldn't imagine. Know how to awaken her impatience, her demand or even her fury. Know how to tease, know how to make her desire rise ever higher, delaying more and more the big moment when you finally explode. If each one falls back exhausted on their side of the bed, then all went well."

Unexpectedly, Nero, who had approached the group and listened to Rolim's discourse, let out a belly laugh that seemed inappropriate to everyone.

"Why are you laughing?" Rolim asked.

Nero didn't stop his bellowing. He looked at Rolim, his puny body hidden in the enormous uniform, the cap with 444 in white pulled down to his ears, his little face now bearing an indescribably shocked expression owing to the laughter.

"Ha, what a man! Listening to you, you sound like a professor, but looking at you, you look like a charlatan."

Spiritual Comfort

Doctor Biscaia continued appearing on Sundays to console the prisoners. The funny thing is that in the end, it was not the prisoners who unburdened their troubles, but Doctor Biscaia. He came to take pity on the prisoners, but really it seemed it was the prisoners who took pity on him.

"Have courage, Doctor," said those with whom he normally conversed. "Don't lose your will to live."

This was the situation: For years, Doctor Biscaia's wife had been gravely ill. They said it was sclerosis of the blood platelets, but it wasn't certain if this was a correct diagnosis. The poor woman had not gotten out of bed for a very long time. A lady came to the house to help out with her toilette, but it was Doctor Biscaia who bore the heaviest brunt of the caretaking. Living in that house was a nightmare. Maybe that's why he spent his Sunday mornings at the penitentiary, to do good as the Vincentian that he was.

Apart from the small number of people Doctor Biscaia actually helped, in general the prisoners showed no sympathy for him. They didn't appreciate his perambulating amongst them like the lord of the land, his hat on his head and his saccharine, lowered voice, and that apparently discreet pose that nevertheless indicated that he knew he was being observed as he handed over the church ladies' ounces. The Doctor would certainly have been disappointed if he could have heard the names by which the prisoners among themselves addressed him.

Besides those he had helped, the Doctor talked to others with charitable words. There were quite a few, almost always the same prisoners. Truth be told, they conversed with him for three reasons. Either they felt flattered, as though it were a distinction talking with a person who in their eyes was so important. Or because it was always worth the bother of a conversation in order to receive an ounce, as was the case with Old Lady-Killer. Or because they retained the illusion that Doctor Biscaia, for what he represented and for the connections he enjoyed in the prison, might one day do something for them.

Naturally, hearing his own complaints about life, they said words of consolation to him. The Doctor particularly enjoyed talking with 333 whenever he found him. 333 listened to him attentively, accompanying the complaints with a respectful, approving nod. And at the end, he always had appropriate words.

"God knows your suffering, Doctor Biscaia. But we can't go against the will of God. Man's suffering redeems him from his sins, and through his kindness and devotion, he will receive eternal reward."

Doctor Biscaia also nodded his head. It looked like he believed.

Love Letters

Nazaré now was in no hurry to leave his cell. Frequently, at recreation time, he'd say to the guard he wasn't feeling well and asked to stay. They figured he was sick, and they left him there. But no, he wasn't sick. The sickness, if that's what you could call it, was something else.

The best moments for him now were those he spent locked in his cell. He read and reread the letters he received from 31's sister. And the time passed quickly rereading them, and writing, correcting and editing his letters in response.

Locked in his cell, he didn't hear the horrible noise of the prison routine. He heard nothing. He dreamt of the future, spending hours imagining it. His were serious thoughts, projects and plans that little by little he constructed with care and discipline, everything he hoped for down to the most minute details. At the wedding, he'd wear black, and she white, with a long veil and garland of flowers. Confetti would rain down, and rice would be thrown on leaving the church. The house would be newly painted, furnished and arranged, bright as a sunny day.

He imagined everything with the clean thoughts that steadily grew in his mind. So much so that when the flow of his imagination led him to envision the big moment of intimacy with her as a woman, he fled from the specter of her feminine nakedness and physical closeness that almost offended him, and that inevitably ended his every train of thought.

By now, the worst part of his time in prison wasn't the prison itself but the slow waiting until that anxious moment when he would go free. His passion was so great that sometimes he felt a surprise attack of terror at losing his beloved.

"My love," he wrote one day. "I know that three years are a lot. A lot for me until that faraway day. A lot for you, too, I know. But it's worth the wait because happiness is awaiting us."

The response he received amazed him. "...three years, my love, are a lot. But what of it? The way I love you, I'd wait five or six...."

Surely an exaggeration, Nazaré thought, or just an expression. In any case, if he felt passionate, why wouldn't she feel that way, too? But beyond that, her expression was so captivating, so generous, that it ignited the flames of passion.

Months after that letter, when it came time for another visit with 31, he tried to read in the girl's face what the letters revealed to him. In the shadow of the neighboring visiting booth, he could barely discern her features. But slyly, he was certain of it, he perceived a look from her, sweeter than ever.

Escorted by the guard, Nazaré and 31 returned to their cells. On the way, he whispered a comment. "It's hard waiting, pal," he admitted frankly.

Only several steps later did 31 answer.

"Whoever waits will surely get there, friend. You fell into a big piece of luck, what more do you want?"

"Shhhhh!" the guard hissed to silence them.

That 31 is awful, Nazaré thought. *He doesn't feel things. For sure he was never in love.*

Little Friar's Innocence

It was authorized to have a portable gasoline stove or an alcohol lamp in your cell to cook or heat up whatever you wanted. Catalan had a lamp. One afternoon, a little before the count-off, with the door cells still open, he saw that he was out of alcohol. He went to the guard and asked if he could still get a prisoner-aide to go buy some at the canteen.

Rinaldo, on duty, didn't answer at first. Immobile as a tame bull, he heard Catalan without even looking up.

"No, no you can't," he answered coldly.

What a pissy response. The canteen was still open, and what Catalan was asking was clear enough; usually, authorization was given. He asked again.

"No!" Rinaldo repeated, and with a solid, heavy step, walked away.

Catalan retreated to his cell muttering. No sooner did one of his neighbors, who had heard the conversation, appear at the door. It was Little Friar. Small and humble, he walked bent over, his hands together as if he were praying as he went. He had been convicted for rape, but he always affirmed his innocence. "If you want, I can get a flask for you."

Catalan accepted. Little Friar left, and after a short while returned with a full flask.

Catalan saw the blue of the denatured alcohol and gratefully paid three or four times the price. Little Friar knew that for Catalan money was no problem. A little later, the guards whistled, proceeded to the count-off and, with the usual clamor of locks and bolts, closed the cell doors.

Then Catalan received a surprise. Lighting the alcohol in the lamp, *pffft!* a quick spark and then out. He tried one, twice, three times and always the same thing happened. *Pffft!*, a spark, and out.

Little Friar had concocted some mixture and sold it to Catalan as the real thing. No one knew anything about this mixture, but the profit was real. Catalan didn't complain, however, because it was prohibited to conduct business with other prisoners. It also wasn't possible to handle the issue directly, because even though Little Friar was in the next cell, he'd always slip out.

Until one day, when Catalan grabbed him right in front of his door, practically pushing his big belly into him, and looked at him threateningly: "You did a filthy thing. You are a goat," he said, his voice trembling in his Spanish-laced Portuguese.

Little Friar was not upset. "You are mistaken," he responded quite gentlemanly. "The stuff was the best. Very good. *Muy bueno.*"

A furious Catalan turned his back on him and entered his own cell like a hurricane, producing a gust with the removal of his corporeal bloat.

The incident became known. One Sunday at mass, 333 took Little Friar to task. He felt comfortable doing so because these two were both among the most devout.

"You shouldn't have done it, brother. God could punish you."

"No, He won't, brother," Little Friar answered. "I am innocent." His eyes had an expression of such humility that it was hard not to believe him.

"All the better that you are innocent," said 333.

"All the better that you believe me," Little Friar concluded.

333 knew much about life and humanity. Little Friar just showed that he knew no less.

The New Director

It was big news for the prisoners when the director of the penitentiary, Martins-Lucas, as the prisoners called him, was replaced by a new director, a young lawyer and nephew of the minister of justice. It could have been considered just a cushy job—but no. The new director had a sleeve full of good intentions and almost revolutionary reforms for prison life.

He eliminated the cap. He eliminated the big numbers formerly emblazoned on the prisoners' back, pants and cap, and exchanged them with a small strip with the respective number attached at the chest. It almost looked like a decoration. He increased recreation time. He started having audiences with prisoners. He created a communal hall for prisoners on the path toward rehabilitation. And, according to word of mouth, he gave decisive orders to improve the food and do away with corporal punishment under any circumstances.

The new uniforms were delayed in arriving, but when they did, they were a success. No big numbers, bare heads. In their new apparel, the prisoners felt respected. They felt indisputably better.

Opinions about these measures varied among the guards. Ernesto, for example, in support of the new director, said that before now, all was not right and that something had to be done. Bazuca, to the contrary, called the whole thing asinine, insisting that the new director was still very young and had no experience. He blurted out his criticisms so crassly that his colleagues distanced themselves, so as not to be compromised. Rinaldo, hearing his colleagues, uttered not a peep. It did not need saying that the order henceforth forbidding corporal punishment would not apply to Rinaldo. About one thing all the guards complained: Without the big numbers on their backs and caps, the prisoners played cat and mouse games, escaping amongst the others without being able to be identified.

As for the prisoners, there were no dissenting opinions: The new director was right. As far as is known, there was only one less enthusiastic note, from 402.

He just said, "This won't last long."

Meals and Delicacies

After the new director started on the job, the meals improved. Of course, there was still a good quantity of rancid oil in the storeroom that had to be used up. The same with the beans hard as rocks for having taken on water in storage. In compensation, that revolting fish with the ugly name, usually served once or twice a week, disappeared for a while. Less frequent, too, were the burned, crushed bread crusts only good for throwing out.

Little by little, all through the prison, whenever the occasion arose, the changes spilled out into conversations about fun old times and regional foods.

"There's nothing better than a shad empanada," said the convict Porto Alto, proud of the River Tagus marshland he came from.

"No way," Falua answered. "I tried it and it's nothing but bread and bones."

"You tried a bad imitation," Porto Alto replied. "Or else whoever made it didn't know how. If it's well made, you wouldn't find a single bone."

333 listened and smiled, but said nothing.

Nazaré walked around deeply absorbed in his correspondence with 31's sister. He circled about the recreation area, alone and thoughtful. But he couldn't contain himself, passing by one group, when he heard what he considered a preposterous phrase: "Sea snake? You don't eat sea snake."

"Could I say something?" he dared to intrude in the conversation. "You're surely talking about moray. It looks like sea snake, but it isn't. Ugly, yes, but—"

"Just looking at it makes you throw up," the other interrupted.

"It might be ugly, but it's delicious. You just need to slice it thin and fry it well until it's toasted just right. You eat it all."

Joining the conversation, Elvas told how the vagrant workers prepare pork.

"First, they go to a farm. They choose one of the smallest pigs. They give it ground glass with something to eat, and the pig swallows it down greedily. The next day, it can't stop grunting, screeching and shitting blood. The managers decide it has some disease and they bury it. Under wraps, that night the guys go and dig up the pig and begin working. Washed well and rolled in clay that they've already prepared, they place it to roast over a big fire. It takes a while, but it cooks. Then they take it off the fire, break off the clay and throw it away, cut off the choice pieces and pack them in until they're gorged."

"But they can't eat the whole pig," the others agreed.

"It's not meant to," Elvas answered. "They stuff themselves with what they like and bury the rest to cover their tracks."

Each one spoke of the delicacies of their region as though they were the best in the world. For those from Porto it was pork tripe stew. For those from the northeast, bean stew à la Transmontana. For those from Alentejo, lamb stew, empanadas, fried bread, gazpacho. Those from the Algarve liked their fish with lemon, potatoes topped with corn flour, clam chowder and so forth.

Everyone agreed on two undebatable dishes: grilled sardines and kale soup.

"And that's why we're Portuguese," Falua whispered jokingly.

Catalan's Workshop

With the yard full of prisoners at recreation, a strange group of civilians appeared, well dressed, wearing ties, accompanied by the head guard and staff from the administration. They marched rapidly alongside the buildings. Opening a door, they disappeared from the prisoners' view.

"What are those guys going to do in Catalan's workshop?" someone asked.

Before anyone could answer, a new surprise: Accompanied by two guards, Catalan was brought to the workshop.

That workshop had gained celebrity and an aura of mystery. The prisoners called it Catalan's workshop. Catalan did not appreciate that—he called it a laboratory. Even back in the time of Martins-Lucas, the former director, they had installed costly equipment with high authorization from Prison Services. Catalan was conducting experiments there to create a new liquid combustible fuel. He was even authorized to give a press conference in which he referred not only to the progress of his research, but to the innovative reforms in the prison system, offering his fellow prisoners a sample of his vast knowledgeability.

From the visit to the workshop that day, it later became known that it had been organized by the prison director and specialists sent by the Prison Services administration.

"Could it be that Catalan has really invented a new combustible?" some asked.

The fact that Catalan had a notable record of swindling and abuses of confidence was a known certainty. At the same time, it could be seen that he was a man of experience, intelligence and invention. Not that his demeanor would have indicated it. He was a bulky man, round and flabby, with tires of fat, double chin and almost deformed goiters. Anyone talking with him forgot all that however. What they saw was a refined, attentive and bright man of fluid, calm and appropriate speech. It would be hard not to believe him.

Even back in Martins-Lucas's time, he had obtained support for setting up the workshop. The new prison director supported it also and, declaring himself confident of success, incorporated the experiment into his innovative plans.

Some prisoners did not share such confidence.

"Here you have the wise man and the fool," said Garino one day. "Catalan is the wise man because he's shining. The fool is the director because he thinks he came here to shine."

On the Common Origin of Animals

Some liked to hear Silvino discourse on animals and nature. Sometimes, however, he traveled so far afield in his excursions of fantasy that he gained the reputation of being slightly lunatic. One day, in his weak, hesitant voice, he spoke of the insects that populated the garden.

"We observe them, we hunt them down, we kill them. But we are made of the same matter and we come from the same source. An Englishman discovered some time back that man descended from the monkey. That is, the monkey, like man, descend from a simian who was grandfather to both. You can believe it's not true if you want, but we are cousins without a doubt."

Those who heard him found that funny. But Silvino was speaking in earnest. Nor did he leave it at that.

"Our family is even far greater," he continued. "Many times you've seen the skeletons of other animals. And you can see photographs of the skeletons of animals that lived thousands and even millions of years ago and have disappeared from the earth. In the library, there's a book with those photos. Ask 333. And haven't you seen with your own eyes the insides of rabbits, dogs, cats, cattle, horses? Just like humans, they have lungs, stomach, liver, kidneys, intestines and all the rest. And the skeletons? The bones? They have skulls, spines, legs, arms, ribs, teeth of different sizes but very similar to those of men."

He paused a moment and went on. "You might think this is nonsense, but it's not. If you consider it well, the whole animal kingdom has physical systems similar to ours. Eyes, mouth, intestines, sex. Even a male fly puts himself into a female fly just like a man. The way I see it, we all come from the same vine."

"And a bedbug? A flea? A louse?" Serpentina interrupted.

Silvino did not respond. If he did, Serpentina would only be surprised all the more, because he posed his questions in jest, assuming a "no" as the correct answer. And Silvino certainly would have answered him with a serious "yes."

Temptation

The Captain never expected this. In the narrow space of the partially opened cell door appeared the prying figure of one of the prisoner-aides who sometimes brought his meals. The lively black eyes in his young face surveyed the cell at a glance and then fixed on the Captain. The young fellow did not enter. Through the door gap only his face could be seen focusing on the space inside.

"What's up?" the Captain asked finally.

"I wanted to ask you a favor, Mister Captain," the words accompanied by a daring, even malicious smile. "It's just a little thing that I ask you out of the respect that I have for you."

Emerging through the semi-opened gap, the head without a body looked like a puppet from some show at a country fair.

"So, what is it?"

"Look, Mister Captain, sometimes I come to your cell to bring you your meal, and you have your watch on top of the table. For the love of God, take your watch off the table. Put it on your wrist, or wherever you want, but take it from the table. Because if you don't do as I ask, one day for sure I'm going to take it," having said which, the head disappeared.

"What an idiot," the Captain grumbled to himself.

He wasn't. He had spoken honestly and with the best of intentions. For, in fact, one day the watch disappeared. The Captain complained to the guards, recalling the aide's words, and demanded that they find the thief. The guards reported the incident to the head guard, who related it to the director, who ordered that the case be resolved. They conducted an investigation but never found the watch, nor who took it.

The Martin and His Mate

The prisoners from B and C wings took their recreation in the big triangular yard at the base of the immense façades of the two wings, each at different times. When those of one wing walked around at recreation, barely discernible faces frequently appeared in one or another grated window on the façade of the other wing. If the guard noticed, he would whistle right away so that those curious figures perched way up behind the grates would go away. This scene repeated itself daily—and month after month, year after year. It was part of the customary routine.

One spring day, during recreation, the C Wing prisoners happened to look up at a unique event.

"Look! Look!" some shouted.

Out of one of the small grated windows on B Wing, an arm extended itself, and then the hand released a little bird which, in rapid flight, as if it wanted to flee from prison, quickly disappeared across the external prison wall and the guard towers.

Every time the men of C Wing went to their recreation, they always carefully looked up at the mysterious barred B Wing window. Among the many dozens of windows on four floors that dotted the enormous length of the faded ochre façade, that was the only one that attracted anyone's attention.

Even those like Catalan or Wild Boar, who pretended never to look at it, couldn't resist throwing a glance in that direction. Many, grouped together, watched and commented. 333, passing by on one of those occasions and not knowing the whole story, couldn't keep from saying, "Swallows, my friends, are the birds of Our Lady—"

"They're not swallows," Garino contested. "It's a martin." Then he added ironically, "So tell us, master. Whose are the martins? Our Lord's?"

333 retreated irritably, quickening his pace. "Blasphemers!" he muttered.

Some heard him and laughed.

The scene repeated itself and gained new contours. The bird had now been identified and was, in fact, a martin. Released from the space behind the grate, it always flew to the right over the wall and the guard towers. After a while it returned, not baffled by the many dozens of windows on the façade, and always made direct aim toward the same grated window it had left from, and where a friendly hand received it.

A few weeks later, a new development: The martin came back accompanied. Now two birds were released to fly, later returning to

the same cell. The observation of these movements and the anticipa-
tion of what would ensue became the favorite activity of the C Wing
prisoners at recreation.

Nero went nuts over them. He stood rooted in place, waiting in the
middle of the yard. When the birds would fly out together, or fly back,
he let out his excited exclamations. "Hey, boys! This is really nifty!"

One day, though, the couple left and did not return. For weeks,
eyes were fixed on the window in hope of again seeing the martins' release and return. Nothing. Neither one nor the other. A vague
sense of sadness overcame the prisoners of C Wing at recreation.
They invented explanations. How could they decipher it?

Only much later, a guard related what happened, though on B
Wing, everyone knew the story. The martin returned with his mate,
and the two happily flew around their friend's accustomed cell. An
error in calculation spoiled everything. Wanting to obtain the same
result with the lady martin, the martin's friend decided to close the
window for the days needed to achieve his goal. The reaction was
unexpected. The surprised couple flew about, nervously shedding
their feathers beating against the window glass and bars, until the
two tired birds settled cowering and tremulous into a corner. When
the prisoner finally, and with little expectation of success, opened
the window, they didn't wait any longer and shot straight away like
arrows over the walls and the guard posts, and disappeared forever.

A Quiet Man

How it happened, no one knew or tried to find out. Maybe because
both of them were pranksters, and one prankster with another
prankster oftentimes does not end well. But in one corner of the
yard, Falua and Serpentina got involved in a fistfight. A blow here, a
punch there, like animals. Before the momentarily distracted guards
could turn around and see what was happening, however, another
prisoner grabbed the two with force and unexpected decisiveness,
separated them and remained standing silently as if nothing had
occurred. It was Gonçalo.

The guards looked over and saw the two of them somewhat out of
sorts, Falua straightening himself out, and Serpentina tucking in his
shirttails. They approached. "What's going on?"

No one answered. The guards looked suspiciously at both of them,
and then walked away.

Meanwhile, Gonçalo melted into the midst of the others. He was
what you would call a quiet man no one noticed. He said little to the

others, and the others never spoke about him. Once in a while, but rarely, he could be seen conversing with Augusto or Garino. Also unknown were where he came from and what crime he had committed. He did everything the others did in the course of prison routine, but no one paid him any attention.

Except that it happened several times that he would appear at fraught moments of conflict, as if he had risen from the ground, so calm, so gentle, so sure and so confident, that the other men—his fellow prisoners, and even the guards—deferred to his magisterial gestures.

The Gynecologist's Crime

They had a special animus toward the prisoner in cell 8 on C Wing. It seemed strange, even, how such universally strong feelings of condemnation, censure, anger and disgust coalesced against him.

Maybe on account of the prayers he spouted in his cell. Of course, there were others who prayed aloud besides him. Every night the voice of the repentant Old Man echoed throughout the immense space: "Forgive me, Lord! Forgive me!"

333, the sacristan-librarian-milk deliveryman, also prayed out loud, but in a more tempered voice and with a lightly discordant note. His displays of devotion couldn't avoid being heard without a slightly perceptible note of irony. Old Man was sincere, no doubt, even allowing for the fact that he had quite a few screws loose.

The prisoner in cell 8 was a different case. A medical doctor by profession, he only assumed his religious fervor when he sensed the guards coming to open his cell door or look through the bullseye. Then he fell to his knees, joined his palms in supplication, looked imploringly above, hoping they would witness his show, and regurgitated prayers with unintelligible words. Maybe because he did not know the catechism, he just improvised the text.

"Enough with this farce!" a guard hurled at him one day opening the door.

As if awakening, he turned to the guard as if nothing unusual had happened. "Mister Guard was saying. . . ?"

Another time, removing the lid off his meal and seeing the dried beans and malodorous fish, he commented to the aide, "Didn't you have anything better to bring me?"

The aide didn't appreciate his manners. "Look, you asshole," he retorted. "Since you asked, I'm going to bring you a pan full of shit you can shove your puss into."

Everyone felt revolted by him.

Despite the many protections he enjoyed, the doctor could not get away with it. He went too far. Repeating his singular exploit over the period of a number of years had become the essence of his life. His game was to choose the most beautiful among the patients who consulted him as a gynecologist. He chose the appropriate time and scheduled their appointment. The rest was easy. He put his patients to sleep and fucked them. With the precautions he used before, during and after, he figured he would never be caught. They would be perfect crimes.

But they weren't. One way or another, suspicions arose, then talk, then complaints and investigations. Numerous cases came to light, and many others would have, too. The clever doctor faced trial with six hundred accusation files on him. Appeals on his behalf poured in; after all, he came from fine parentage, and he had respectable colleagues and friends. Besides which, his crime not only shone a bad light on him, but on the profession, on his social circle, on his class. The court notoriously gave him only six years in the pen.

Now he prayed loudly, never missed a Sunday mass, obeyed the orders he received, and at daily recreation, he kept himself apart and spoke to no one, because he felt he had nothing in common with criminals.

The Cat, a Man of Talent

For many, the Cat was a source of pride, almost a legend. Not for the crime he had committed because, amazing though it may sound, no one spoke of it, but for being recognized as a man of formidable talent.

The first big proof he provided five years ago, when he was employed in the workshop that assembled motorbikes. The model was good but had one defect: The brakes wore away the tires. The manufacturer sent an order to discontinue the assembly because sales were falling off. It was then that the Cat came forward, saying, "I can fix it."

Although dubious, the manager gave him a chance. In fact, the Cat did resolve the problem by creatively altering the braking system.

"The guy knows more than the engineers," his companions said.

The second big proof was a somewhat more complicated job. It's not clear who decided it, but a decision was taken at the highest level, to erect a small monument at the penitentiary to the minister of justice, author of one of many reorganizations of the prison service. His reorganization was neither better nor worse than many others had made in the past. The difference was that the author was still the minister of justice. Glory to those who deserve it!

The bust was commissioned from a high-priced sculptor, cast in bronze in a foundry in the city and finally placed on a stone pedestal in the entrance patio of the prison.

That's where the story would have ended forever if it hadn't also been decided to conduct a solemn inauguration with the presence of the minister and a ceremonial address. The minister showed up, self-important and pleased. Suddenly, he started frowning evermore grimly, giving off signs of restlessness and shuffling his feet and legs so visibly that Prison Director Martins-Lucas asked him softly, "Are you feeling ill, Your Honor?"

The minister didn't respond. He bore up. But at the end of the ceremony, he blew up, and he had his reasons. With the technique the sculptor had employed, the face was not smooth or polished. Rather, in the opinion of His Excellency, it looked streaked with creases and blemishes.

He angrily rejected the thing, and a few days later, the bust was taken down and the matter subjected to reconsideration.

No one knows how it was that the Cat arose to solve the problem. Maybe he offered his expertise, as he had with the bicycle brakes. In any case, he took absolute charge of recasting the bust. To that end, a specially designated little workshop was created for him. Finally there emerged a bust with a face so smooth, polished and shiny that you'd believe the minister, at the very moment when he had posed for the sculptor, had just shaved and splashed on the highest quality aftershave lotion. The re-inauguration was a more modest affair, but to the glory of both minister and Cat, the little monument stayed.

From such achievements he earned admiration. The Cat spoke to everyone directly, to their face. He didn't put distance between himself and others, though they did. They approached him with familiarity, but with restraint.

People whispered that the prison itself and the workshop owners gave him ample rewards. The Cat neither confirmed nor denied it. But it was known, nevertheless, that the bicycle business, as well as the furniture business and another dealing in metalwork that he had contacted him in connection with the minister's bust, all offered him well-paid work when he'd go free in three or four years.

"That guy's not going to have any difficulties when he gets out. He'll get all the work he wants." So people said.

He was one of those rare instances where a prisoner could have fundamental certainty that, after his sentence was over, he'd have a secure job and future.

The Joy of Love

For Nazaré, the days passed more slowly now because on the outside the future was waiting for him. But those same days were brightened by the love that he conveyed to Ivette (that was her name) and that came through the letters he received from her.

Surely, writing is writing, and talking is talking. It's not easy to get to know people only through correspondence. From the start, there was a certain contrast. Nazaré's letters were passionate but restrained, speaking of life and plans. Ivette's letters at times spoke seriously about things and also conveyed perhaps an excess of passion and impatience, even intimacy and shamelessness, that shocked Nazaré a little as they aroused him. "Ay, my boy!" he read in one of them. "Trust that I am a virgin and yearn with every fiber of my body and heart for our marriage night."

Between letters, Nazaré waited for weeks or months for their next visit together. The guards continued to escort him with 31, and as always, they sat in side-by-side visiting booths. Nazaré gave less and less attention to his visiting mother. He did nothing but look over at 31's sister, hoping for a glance back or a gesture. The girl was the soul of discretion. Only once did she smile at him openly, inspiring him to redoubled courage. Heartened, on the next visit several weeks later, assuring himself that the guards weren't looking, he raised his fingers to his lips and blew her a kiss.

31 saw that, and his reaction was not long in coming. "Don't do that," he reprimanded him afterward. "I facilitated things for you, but I don't want trouble. Write what you want, plan whatever you want with her. But at visiting time, it's like nothing's happening."

"Okay, I'm sorry," Nazaré agreed. "If that's the way it has to be, that's the way it will be."

Giving up hope for a little smile or special gesture, he devoured her with his eyes despite the relative darkness of the visiting booth and gave free rein to passion in the letters he wrote.

Three in the Same Line of Work

Argentino, Catalan and the Captain were three very different men, but among them, there was some ineffable trace of commonality that brought them together.

When Argentino started to draw himself toward the two others, they shrank away with reservation. The story of his victim's execution with gunshots from the Colt in the temple and between the eyes gave them goosebumps. Both of them preferred a sweeter kind of killing, but they overcame their problem with him. Argentino was upstanding, used his words well and showed appreciation for their braggadocio. Little by little, he revealed himself to be a fellow specialist in their art.

Catalan and the Captain would relate their feats of prowess. In truth, you couldn't really speak about the Captain's prowess. His robberies and frauds had been many and sizable. Embezzlements, abuses of trust, forged signatures, checks with insufficient funds. Big amounts. But all those had been adjudicated in routine, well-known cases that contributed little to his reputation and prestige.

Catalan was different. The history of his swindles was far greater than his long record indicated—from country to country, one trafficking deal after another, every one of them huge and the object of bold, complex schemes, leaving in their wake shelves of voluminous dossiers of trial documents.

In conversation with them, Argentino held back, though he could well have taught them quite a bit. Some of his feats had achieved distinct notoriety in the press, so sensational and cleverly contrived were they, and often so compromising of highly placed figures. Even independent journalists couldn't help but intimate their barely contained sympathy for him. His transactions, involving such great sums of money, were considered, in penal terms, almost beyond culpability.

For example, his operation of exporting extremely valuable shipments of snake and crocodile skins from Brazil to Europe. It was brilliant. He assumed the false identity of an esteemed, internationally recognized zoologist from an imaginary Scientific Institute with appropriately sealed diplomas, a forged passport and business cards as a university researcher. He elaborated a project to send his team on an expedition to the Amazon, and made contact with the Brazilian authorities. Eager for fame, they endorsed his worthy initiative. He went there with a great hullabaloo. Received with pomp and ceremony at universities, institutes and in influential circles, he became friends with some and greased a lot of others' palms. Then he went to work in the field, leaving with all his equipment, but returning very quietly. That part of his act was always secretive, but he proved that, with the right protection, he could successfully transport to and throughout Europe a true fortune in select merchandise without paying taxes or customs.

Argentino had a lot of such stories. Now, listening to Catalan and the Captain, he spoke mostly about his connections and friendships with big shots. The boasts of his two prison pals brought but a poorly disguised smile to his face.

These swindles, however, did not outshine his notoriety over the cold and horrific premeditated assassination of the business partner who betrayed him.

Yet there was another facet of his life which, if known, would have provided a far greater definition of what he had been and what he was. It was that part of his life that explained why he executed his sleeping partner in cold blood with a blast of 9-mm bullets from a Colt—two final ones, one in the temple, the other between the eyes. That facet would become known in the prison only much later.

Horror and Madness

The Captain stopped for a few moments when another prisoner calmly sweeping the floor came up to him and asked for a light.

The Captain, it was said, prized the honor of the Armed Forces. He allowed no familiarity with the other prisoners except for three: Catalan, who might not be an engineer but swore that he was; 333, for the roles that he played within prison life; and Argentino, more for his magisterial presence than for anything he knew about him.

Still, this new one asking him for a light possessed an air of such peace and goodness that on handing him his lighter, he condescended to ask, "Where are you from?"

"From Estarreja," the new man answered simply.

"What did you do before coming here?" Catalan continued his interrogation.

"I worked in dairy products," he responded without elaboration.

And so the conversation began. Not knowing why, the Captain suddenly showed interest in dairy products and, since that was the man's field, he spoke a great deal about it.

When it was time to go back to their cells, Bazuca, who had been watching them from afar, asked, "So, Mister Captain, Mother-Killer told you everything?"

"Mother-Killer? You mean Old Lady-Killer," the Captain said, having already heard of Old Lady-Killer though he didn't know which one of the prisoners he was.

"No. The guy you were talking to is not Old Lady-Killer, he's Mother-Killer. One day, if I get the chance, I'm gonna take him out."

Then Bazuca related the story. That quiet man with the air of such goodness, who spoke so wisely, killed his own mother. To get rid of the body, he cut her into pieces, which he cured in brine, boxed them up and sent the package by rail to a distant train station with no return address.

In the end, the crime was discovered, and he was sentenced.

And just minutes ago, talking to the Captain about his life and how he was fired from a factory, he said, among other things, "Can you believe it, Mister Captain? To this day, I don't understand why I was fired. I worked like everyone else, I fulfilled my duties, and never in my life did I do harm to anyone."

The Captain was aghast. By profession, he was familiar with many ways and means of killing. Not just one or two, but killing by the thousands, the more the better. Preferably military, but also civilians, women and children when necessary or inevitable. In fact, one of the activities for which he was sentenced had to do with the sale of war materiel. He simply had a profound aversion to murder.

"How horrible!" he exclaimed at the guard's information. "Truly the most horrible crime imaginable."

Bazuca shook his head. "These animals are all alike. If every one of them was wiped out, there'd be no loss."

Other Cases

In general terms, the gravity of a crime does not always correspond to the most serious personality traits in a prisoner. A crime is classified as a homicide. But killers are all different. There are killers who are neither worse nor better than many who never killed anyone and never would. There are others whose dark behavior surpasses the imaginable in a human being, that in and of itself can only be explained by insanity.

Besides Old Lady-Killer, there were others. 158 so badly disfigured the face of his victim with a hatchet he figured her identity could never be determined. 225 coldly killed a child at random, with no apparent motive. And many others. Of all the cases known in prison, that of the Lizard was the one that most caused people to shudder.

Even those prisoners accused of very cruel acts looked upon him as if they didn't know him. As if he weren't a man but a repugnant creature such as he appeared: a cold and slimy white lizard.

He did look like one. Someone even suggested calling him the White Lizard. But he wound up being known as just the Lizard. Colorless hair, eyebrows, eyelashes and beard, a whitewashed skin with reddish splotches suggesting sunburn, strands of white hair peeking out from his cap, his glance the fixed glare of the dead, and slow, mechanical movements. He hardly spoke or reacted, but when he did, it was with unexpected discernment. The court found him responsible for his actions. He circled around the prison, broom in one hand, a pail in the other. Whether he swept or not, no one could tell.

By general consensus, the Lizard's crime was the darkest of all those known. On the rare occasions when people made comparisons, the Lizard always took first prize.

In a few words, because any further words would only detract from the story, he killed his wife when he found out she had deceived him. He disemboweled the cadaver, tore out the liver, cooked it up in strips and, when his adolescent children came home for lunch, gave it to them to eat. They were surprised by the treat, on a weekday no less, finding its taste strange, but continued eating without suspecting anything. According to the best-known version of the story, at the end of the lunch, he revealed that they had just eaten their mother's liver. And according to that same version, one of them went crazy, while the other was so emotionally stricken that he died on the spot.

Now the Lizard dragged himself along, expressionless, with the broom in his hand. He spoke to no one, and no one spoke to him.

"The place for a rat like him is not here," Silvino remarked. "He belongs in an insane asylum."

Garino had a more radical view. "For that, only the death penalty. A guy like that shouldn't be walking on this earth. To call him a man is an insult to all of us."

The Fifteen-Centimeter Fistula

For quite a long time, Catalan had been complaining about hemorrhoids and a mean anal fistula that truly bothered him much for the worse because he was a heavy monster of fat pulp. From time to time, they gave him a tube with some kind of ointment, but soon he'd use it up and return to how he was.

Surprising though it may sound, it was his good luck that the old doctor who tried to do what he could went away, and poor Doctor Barnabé arrived. With Doctor Barnabé there now, the nurse received a *de facto* promotion, acting many times as doctor.

Desperate from pain, Catalan tried again and went to the medical office. The first times he had no luck. "Thish'll pash" was, per usual, the response.

It didn't pass, and it continued to hurt, so Catalan pursued another route. He didn't lack for resources, so he bribed the nurse, and the nurse scheduled an appointment.

What Doctor Barnabé did not know, the nurse did: that some tiny wires exist that are inserted into the fistula to determine their depth and angle. Catalan paid well and the nurse suggested their use to Barnabé. "You could probably see it better with a probe, don't you think, Doctor?"

"A pwobe? Whatsh that?"

The nurse explained, Barnabé solemnly nodded his head, Catalan spread himself on the examining table with his immense pink butt cheeks facing into the air, and the nurse prepared to do the probe.

"Shee here, I'll do thish," said Barnabé.

The nurse still made a move to try and do the exam himself, but the doctor, with sudden, rare decisiveness, did it himself.

"Pash it to me, shon," he ordered.

Inserting, then withdrawing the probe, he measured the depth of the fistula with surprising mastery.

"Holy cow!" said the shocked nurse, "fifteen centimeters! One of these days you'd wind up with two holes!"

Considering who he was—Catalan was not just anyone—and the urgency of the situation, the director moved the case forward and the operation was performed. Surprise! It was much easier than predicted. The fistula was only three centimeters long, and Catalan wound up with his bottom like new.

But from the start, there was never an explanation for why the result of Doctor Barnabé's exam was fifteen millimeters.

Intrigued, next time he had the chance, Catalan asked the nurse to explain how the exam showed a depth of fifteen centimeters and, in the end, the surgeon said it was only three.

"Don't tell anyone," the nurse told him in confidence, "but Doctor Barnabé didn't put the probe into the fistula, but straight up your ass!"

Forecasting the Weather

As summer drew near, Silvino got worse, and they brought him again to an infirmary cell. Some days, he stayed in bed; other days, he got up for recreation hour.

Now a sick prisoner whom no one had seen before came in. Benjamim, the infirmary aide, started talking with him, and the fellow spoke about himself with some pride. He was no less than director, editor, publisher and owner of a news sheet called *The Sower*, with a circulation of thousands of copies. Indispensable, according to him, to anyone who worked in agriculture. It taught everything one needed to know. Not just sowing, as the name of the paper suggested, but planting, plowing, weeding, irrigating, cleaning, pruning, fertilizing, grafting, the culture of wine and table grapes, everything in it was discussed with deep knowledge, including the correct time for each phase of work, recommendations for the right manure for different lands, and productivity and profitability.

More than that, the paper—the only one of its kind in Portugal—published the weather forecast a year in advance. Month by month, rigorously confirmed. Such predictions were of vital importance to farmers, as one can readily understand.

Silvino learned all this, and at the first opportunity, at recreation, he cornered the man, who confirmed the information he had given Benjamim.

Silvino knew about the seasons of the year, the equator and the tropics, the equinoxes and the solstices, lunar months and the phases of the moon, the phenomena of the attraction of the moon and the sun, trade winds and anti-trade winds, cyclone and anti-cyclone centers. But he knew nothing that would allow you to predict the weather for each month of the coming year.

He asked the guy how he did it, and the fellow opened up frankly and with obvious conviction. It was simple. As an example, he took the month of July of last year. The first of July tells you about January of the following year, the second about February and so on, until the twelfth day for December. On each of those days, you carefully study the weather and, according to what the weather is like, you make your prediction.

"Nonsense," Silvino couldn't help saying.

"It's always right," the guy responded without reservation.

The conversation took place in June, and as July approached, Silvino proposed to the man to run the experiment right there if he was still around. The man agreed, and a few weeks later, the experiment took place.

On the first day of July, they met at recreation. Silvino arrived on time; the other came late but he showed up. It was a real summer day—hot, blue sky, dry atmosphere. It didn't seem like a promising day to predict the weather for next January. They got together to talk.

"So?" Silvino asked.

The man stopped to look at the sky without losing his composure. "Wait," he answered.

He started walking alongside Silvino without pausing, continuing to look at the sky. Thus, he spent almost the whole recreation hour without announcing his prediction for January of the following year.

Recreation was almost over and Silvino persisted one last time. "So, my friend, what's your forecast?"

With affected solemnity, the man stopped and intently studied the sky from one end to the other. All blue. But just over the horizon above the prison wall, he saw a spreading, but tenuous, ashy blur of feeble haze.

"What are you going to write in your paper?"

"Easy," the man responded categorically. "The sky indicates signs of precipitation. Probable rain."

"Good!" was all that Silvino could say.

The man left and went back to one of the wings. Two years passed before Silvino saw him again, in the infirmary.

He couldn't resist asking him, with barely disguised irony, "So, was your forecast correct?"

"It was, indeed, my friend. Now it's my nephew who's publishing the newspaper and they still sell thousands of copies."

Silvino said no more. Talking with Augusto later, he unburdened himself. "There are people who believe everything. Even what they know is not true. Even their own lies."

God, Sodom and Gomorrah

"There's not a square centimeter on a woman's body that doesn't respond to a caress. If a woman shows disinterest, don't ask for everything. Ask her for only one square centimeter of her body. Her choice, whatever it might be. If she gives it to you and you know how to work it, later you'll get all that you want."

So Rolim lectured in one of his usual speeches. He was totally engrossed in his own oratory when one of his listeners shot a direct question at him, which produced laughter from the others.

"That's all very well and good, but answer me: Did you ever eat pussy?"

333 was passing by and stopped to listen; his ears perked up.

"Saying those words corrupts everything," Rolim answered.

"Did you or didn't you?" the cheeky man insisted.

"Many would not admit to it," Rolim explained. "The truth is that for the man as for the woman, and for the woman as for the man, it's among the purest and highest pleasures. Naturally, there's also a science to it."

"Screw science," the man interrupted. "It's filth, that's what it is."

Rolim did not give up. "If the man and woman are healthy, clean and normal, it's only on account of frigidity, ignorance, prejudice or cowardice that they don't do it."

An indignant 333 separated himself from the group and continued performing his duties.

The direction of the conversation broadened out. Now that they were talking about these things, one of the group, normally quiet, decided to speak up about this issue that had long bothered him:

"I was craving it, I tried, and she resisted like a wild goat. But I did it. The worst was afterward. She insulted me, she got so angry she poisoned our future together, and we wound up separating."

"You didn't know how to do it," Rolim pronounced.

Naturally, they wanted to know how to do it. Rolim explained the preparations, the necessary touches, the attentive observation of reactions, patience and, finally, the moment of attack with acceptance and the feeling of safety.

"Enough of this, man, I can't take any more," one of the group broke in.

During the course of the long explication, a young man who had recently transferred from Monsanto arrived at the gathering. Someone said he was a pickpocket, but a pickpocket wouldn't have earned a sentence at the penitentiary. He must surely have been convicted of something else. Now, for his second time at the group, he listened closely and silently to what everyone said. This time, unexpectedly, he interrupted Rolim:

"Hey, old man! You're like one of those people who eat grilled sardines with a knife and fork. You don't even sound Portuguese when you talk, man!"

And in a chain of vulgar synonyms, he poured out his version of everything Rolim had been expressing in carefully chosen terms.

"Talk Portuguese, man, so we can understand you."

At that, Rolim became irritated. "Just the other day, someone else said the same thing. And that's how everything gets dirty. Besides, you come from Monsanto, and over there it seems they don't even like women. It's all faggotry."

"Okay, boss, now you're finally talking Portuguese. And here? I've been here just a few days, and already they're telling me it's almost everyone. Locked in their cells I don't know how they do it, but that's what they tell me. Look at these folks, man, take a good look and tell me who's not."

People in the group did not like these words. They knew, however, that such things happened. Only a few days before, a guard saw a young fellow leaving Nero's cell, walking quickly with his uniform in disarray, running to escape into his own cell. People heard about it later. Ever since that kid had arrived at the prison—blond, delicate skin, boyish manner—right away the slurs and assumptions began to rain. Nero was the one who took action. He caught him in the passageway, pulled him with a slap into his cell, and with a razor pointed at his throat, he lowered his pants and forced him.

333 returned to the group on his way back. It was hard to guess from his stone face what he thought of what he heard. Finally, he got it off his chest, gruffly but paternal: "Ay, my sons, how shameful. It was for that and other things that God destroyed Sodom and Gomorrah."

And appearing angry, he walked away.

End of the Reforms

Without warning, the new director ended his reforms less than two years after implementing them. The only one salvaged was the communal hall, although experience showed it hadn't been one of the more successful improvements.

One of the measures was the audiences with prisoners who requested them. One day a week, from five to fifteen minutes. They'd sign up, go to the office accompanied by a guard and explain their problem.

Serpentina signed up.

In the space of a few days, he had suffered two violent attacks. In the first one, the convulsions had been so sudden and powerful that three aides, among them Benjamim, who weighed more than a hundred kilos, couldn't control that long, bony, tense body, which bent and unbent twisting in odd angles and pounding the unforgiving cement floor in a succession of jolts. In the second attack, he bit his tongue so hard that once recovered, he could hardly talk. He was petitioning to be transferred to a hospital, and the director saw him.

Calm and collected, Serpentina related what had happened and made his request.

Also calmly, the director responded, "I understand your request very well, young man. But you are better off here than in a hospital prison. After all, here you have recreation, and there you'd be locked in the infirmary. Besides, epilepsy is a terrible disease for which there is no cure. It's not worth your going anywhere else."

"I can't take it in my cell any longer," Serpentina interjected with a slight tone of impatience.

"The cell system is best for you and for the other prisoners. You're tranquil there, and if you have an attack, at least you don't make a spectacle of it in front of the others."

"Bullshit!" Serpentina murmured.

"I see you don't agree," said the director, "but what can I do?"

"Bullshit, bullshit, bullshit!" Serpentina continued, his voice rising.

"I'm sorry, but what do you want? That I somehow make your illness disappear?"

"Bullshit!" Serpentina growled.

That's when the tempest broke. His whole body started moving like a steel spring released from intense pressure. In one fell swoop his arm swept everything off the director's desk, scattering papers, files, an oil lamp and a vase full of flowers to the floor. Then, as the director sat shocked and paralyzed, and the guard looked on incredulously, he set upon a cabinet with glass doors. It's hard to grasp how in such brief seconds, in a fury of movements against the cabinet, everything was smashed and scattered.

More guards came, overpowered Serpentina, battered him with clubs, brought him to a cell in the infirmary and strapped him into a straitjacket.

He fell asleep and when he awakened, peaceful again, he could not explain what had happened. He claimed he remembered nothing of it. With genuine surprise, he felt his painful black bruises.

As for the director, he immediately canceled the prisoner auditions, and for unknown related reasons, started one by one killing off the prison reforms that up to that point he had proudly invoked as the purpose for which he had accepted the job. The old uniforms and caps came back with the big numbers overlaid in white. The old mess reappeared, the indigestible fish and the dried beans hard as rocks.

There was also no explanation why soon after, without any other factors coming into play, they closed Catalan's workshop. After almost two years of support and investment, they came to realize what the majority of prisoners had already accepted as proven fact, because among them, the scam was well known: that Catalan had bamboozled everyone with the supposed invention of a new fuel. The prison administration came down hard. In the director's long, documentary report, he levied against Catalan the punishment of no visitors for one month.

The prisoners interpreted this decision in their own manner, but some of them knew—because he himself had said it—that Catalan was not expecting any visitors that month. In other words, the director himself was also part of the scheme, and now he was finished with Catalan and needed to cover his ass.

Paying for the Damage, Naturally

Serpentina was summoned to the head guard's office. When he left it, furious and needing to vent to someone, he went straight to Benjamim.

"You want to know something? Are they nuts or what? Are they telling me now I have to pay for what I damaged in the director's office? Are they saying I have to go slave in one of their workshops?"

"That's the law," Benjamim said. "The same happened with Nero. They want him to go work in the furniture shop to pay for the damages he made in his cell after he left isolation."

"I'm not even sure what I did," Serpentina replied. "From what they tell me, between what I broke and the misery wage they pay in the workshops, I could be working the rest of my life and wouldn't pay off the damage."

"Yes, I know they pay a miserly wage. But you get to breathe a little air, and they always give you a few pennies. It's better than spending year after year locked in your cell."

"They're not getting me," Serpentina protested. "Let the other jerks work."

"You could be forced, man. It's the law," Benjamim insisted.

They both went to talk with Silvino. "Yes, there's a law," he confirmed. "The law is bad, but even so, they don't obey it. Here's Serafim, who's worked for years as an aide doing jobs around the prison. The law says for prison service, you can only work three months a year. And you, Serpentina, what are you going to get out of making furniture? The law says prisoners who work should earn the same as they'd earn for the same work on the outside. It's a lie. The law says prisoners who work are entitled to the same rights concerning work accidents. Another lie. 88 lost three fingers and never received a cent. You can work if you want. If you don't want to work, no one can force you. They can harass you, but they can't force you."

A few days later, Serpentina was called once again to see the head guard, who repeated that he needed to work to pay off the damage. Serpentina listened, listened, all the while getting more upset, and then he growled. "Bullshit!"

The guard who led him to the chief guard was the same one who had conducted him to the director when that violent incident occurred. Remembering that growl that preceded the wild outburst, the guard said a few words into the chief's ear.

"It's all right, it's all right. Take the man away," the chief ordered. After they left, he mumbled, "I don't know anymore if this is a prison or a madhouse."

Revolt on B Wing

No one ever explained the reasons. The only witness to the start of it all said he had seen Bazuca going toward Malveira with a raised club and suddenly receiving a crushing blow on his head from the broom that Malveira wielded. He fell hard to the floor, his head all bloody. The blow hit him squarely with the broom's heavy metal hoop.

For a few seconds, everything stood still: Malveira in place, glancing quickly from one side to the other, Bazuca, sprawled on the floor, a prisoner observing the scene, glued to his spot.

Suddenly, everything flew into action. Repeated alarm whistles screeched from the rotunda. Prisoners appeared at their cell doors to glimpse what was happening. And as Bazuca stood up, huffing but having pulled himself together, the metal grate sounded violently, and then, like a hurricane, half a dozen guards swarmed into the wing.

Malveira waited, stiff and motionless, but when the guards came running and got near him, he raised the broom in a dizzying whirl and with quick, calculated moves made a circle hitting and felling two or three guards. Some of the prisoners who had come to see entered the fray, and a royal battle ensued. Malveira and the other insurrectionists were conquered in the end. The revolt had been insti-gated by Rinaldo and Bazuca, and they gave it to them really hard, blindly kicking bodies and heads. Despite being beaten, bloody and barely conscious, they continued getting thrashed the whole time.

"Enough!" said the guard Ernesto finally, placing himself in front of Rinaldo, who looked like a mad bull in his violent thrusts.

It stopped. If the beatings had continued, none of the prisoners would have been left alive.

At the end, the guards mobilized other prisoners to carry the wounded down to basement isolation, one in each cell.

For several days, no one else had access to the basement. Ben-jamim from the infirmary was tasked with bringing the mess trays down to the punished.

"So?" his companions asked him when he returned.

Benjamim said nothing. Except a few days later, meeting Garino, he spoke. "I never saw anything like it. Everyone looked like a bloody pulp. They didn't even call the nurse or Barnabé. Those bastards should be shot, dammit."

Weeks passed. One day, the aide received no instruction to take meals to the isolation ward prisoners. No one ever saw them again in the penitentiary. Surely, they were transferred out—in the middle of the night.

Year After Year

Some years remain marked by major events: an escape, a revolt, a homicide, a higher-than-average number of suicides, or even by less spectacular events that also entered the annals of real or imaginary history. Worst of all, the other years unraveled in the terrible, cruel routine of punishing men.

With this or that rare exception, the days passed alike, with the same rules, the same motions, the same rituals. The whistles, the waking, the noisy echo of opening cells, the emptying of buckets, the stink of shit and creosol, the count-off, the slither of clogs and slippers, the distribution of coffee and a crust of bread, again the slamming of locks and bolts, the isolation in the cells, the inner silence, the tedious sounds of distributing the lunch trays, the spread of the smell of fish fried in rancid oil or of the musty kale soup, the whistles, the lineup, the recreation, the whistles, the lineup, the return to the cells, once again the racket of locks and bolts at distribution time for dinner, the diffusion of nauseating smells, and more whistles, and the final count-off, more locks and bolts, and then the silent hour, the isolated sounds, and the humid, chilly atmosphere as the shadows advanced at end of day into darkness of night.

As always, day after day, 210 reciting aloud the countdown of time passed and time still to serve. The years, months and days already endured in prison, and the years, months and days of prison still to suffer. The count offered daily, rigorously correct, in a loud voice.

And as always, day after day, week after week, month after month, year after year, evermore weak and imploring, the voice of the Old Man at prayer during the hour of silence:

"Forgive me, Lord! Forgive me!"

With slight variations, the last noises in the approaching sepulchral quietude were lonely complaints, sighs, coughing jags; the bare, strong bang of the rotunda gate letting who knows who through. Then everything remained still like a gigantic tomb until the lively wakeup the next morning.

"Have you noticed," Garino asked Augusto one day, "how awful it is being here? It's such an effort to get through each day, sometimes you just want to do something stupid. Then you think about it a little and you wonder at the passage of so many years."

The Grand Seigneur Vianinha

If you saw him or heard him, you'd think nothing of him. Puny, sober, expressionless, always speaking in a low voice, he would go unnoticed if he weren't so famous, for he was a personality with real power in that environment. No one spoke of what he had done on the outside, but here, he was king of the black market.

He sold items you couldn't find in the canteen: cigarettes, razor blades, shaving cream, bars of soap, mechanical pencils, everything naturally at prices two or three times the current market. Everything on order. For select buyers, he could also get photos of naked women, pornographic magazines and even small doses of hashish. And he practiced another, more lucrative activity, for a very modest reward. For example, the loan of a hundred *escudos* payable in two weeks, with another ten *escudos* interest. It didn't seem like a lot for someone who needed it that much. Risk is risk, and commands its price. Vianinha knew how to do business, and an interest rate of two hundred to five hundred percent did not seem excessive.

Such activities were widely known. No one was surprised by them. Although, as a humble person, he conducted his transactions and business with circumspection, always speaking in his naturally quiet voice, without haste or insistence, the great number of people who sought him out and the curious looks of the others had transformed Vianinha into a true institution.

Many times, he was openly seen. He was spotted by prisoners and guards entering Catalan's cell with a package and casually leaving the package behind. He was witnessed talking with this one and that one, exchanging things, receiving money. To top it off, he was seen coolly approaching the guard on watch duty at recreation and stopping next to him without a word. Vianinha's and the guard's hands touched, and Vianinha resumed his leisurely walk.

Porto Alto observed the action. "Now everything is done in broad daylight," he said to the mate beside him.

People wondered how he could act with complete impunity. From where and how did he access these articles? Where did he keep or hide them? Why did they never search his cell? Why did the guards pretend not to see these activities? What could he have done to be so scandalously protected?

On their own or in conversation, prisoners asked such questions. No one asked Vianinha. He was evidently playing his officially recognized part and was undeniably hard to dispense with.

Rinaldo Gets It

At times, the veterans tussled with Falua. Many there were whose extremely serious crimes had made history—homicides, armed assaults, dangerous robber gangs—but not Falua. He always acted alone. Just little things, but a lot of them.

"You're a disgrace," 509 (Wild Boar) said to him one day, regarding him with disgust. "You really didn't do much of anything, and you're here like any of us."

Falua didn't disagree, but answered, "You're the one who never did much, pal. You killed someone and they sentenced you right away. What else? I did more than twenty break-ins, was arrested several times, and this time they threw the book at me. And you?"

Holding back for a few seconds, as if expecting a response while glaring daringly at the colossus, he added in an even more delicate, sly tone than his usual, "So in the end, it's me who can say to you, you're a disgrace because you didn't do much but you're here in prison like any of us."

Those who observed the scene thought that with the brute force he had, 509 wouldn't contain himself and would destroy the poor Falua.

But no. Instead, 509 looked his challenger up and down and saw him as so fragile and insignificant that he simply spat to one side and walked away.

Falua was beyond repair however. That's how he was and always would be. He liked to tease and enjoyed making fun of people. He let his taunts fly with his falsetto voice like someone throwing stones wrapped in tissue paper. It was hard not to find him amusing. It was also hard, if he miscalculated whom he was toying with, to avoid vexing them. The majority of the guards didn't take to him. One day, perhaps inspired and prompted by what had gone down with 509, Falua had the unfortunate idea of playing around with Rinaldo. Inevitably, he figured wrong.

Imposing and massive as a bull, Rinaldo had a curious peculiarity. If a prisoner asked him if he could do this or that, he'd immediately say no. This happened with Catalan and many others. But if they asked him in the negative, he'd respond yes.

"Mister Rinaldo, can I go order some more cigarettes from the canteen?"

"No way," he'd answer grimly and in a foul mood, shaking his head in a sign of disapproval.

"Mister Rinaldo, I couldn't go order some cigarettes at the canteen, I don't suppose."

"Yes, you could," Rinaldo responded in that same imposing air.

Falua employed that trick once, twice, ten times and always got positive responses. Until one day Rinaldo caught on to the game, and the jig was up.

"Mister Rinaldo, I wouldn't be able to go to Porto Alto's cell to return the lighter he lent me, I don't guess."

Unlike what happened all the other times, Rinaldo shot him such a look and a frown that Falua understood that the guard finally got it. He felt the blood freeze in his veins and for good reason. In an instant, Rinaldo grabbed him by the shoulders with his enormous burly hands and shook him violently as you'd shake an olive tree to make the olives fall.

"Listen, you scoundrel! Who do you think you're dealing with, huh?" And he called out for another guard.

In a matter of minutes, Falua found himself brutally shoved into a dark isolation cell in the basement, dumped onto the cement.

There he stayed for several days, but it remained to be seen if he would lose his good sense of humor.

Two Hundred Portraits of Women

Argentino's essential life had taken place years before the homicide for which he was sentenced, and also in Portugal. The great revelation came much later.

Arriving in Portugal for the first time, so far as anyone knows, he had the bad luck to be arrested by chance in a routine raid of cabarets in Lisbon. All the patrons in a corner were making a clamor, hands up, holding identification papers. They found Argentino lacking a visa in his passport. That itself was not such a serious thing, but when they searched his hotel suite, a surprise was awaiting them.

Argentino had in his possession nearly two hundred photos of women, young and mostly pretty. On the back, first names—no family names and no other identification—and a number, almost certainly their age, true or fictitious.

This find led to a search of his engagement book. That brought forth new revelations: lists of residences and telephone numbers in Brazil, France and Italy; none in Argentina. As to Portugal, on a separate page, the names of highly placed individuals whom the police considered as having nothing to do with the case, naturally. Some addresses led investigators to expensive brothels restricted to carriers of entrance cards that the customers themselves distributed. Two of them produced fertile leads. In luxury hotels, they found three beautiful young women, one French and two Italians, who had recently arrived. They were en route to enter the Brazilian market. Pressed by the police, they finally informed them that it was Argentino who managed and paid for everything. They also told how he had recently sent a Portuguese woman to Brazil, who had soured on the prospect, was afraid, and tried to escape and return. They feared that the network, if they found her, would liquidate her.

Trafficking in white women had been Argentino's business for years and years. All that time he had invented, owned and operated the white slave market, with its web of kidnappings, private jails, rapes, torture and killing. But he was only suspected. No definitive proof. Four court cases over the years in different countries: four acquittals.

Arrested in Lisbon with the two hundred photos, he extricated himself this time, too. Among his specialties, he would supply—for a pretty price, of course—young women he advertised as demure or married, even in some cases virgins, for the orgies of ministers and other bigwigs in the dictatorship. Once again, his experience showed him the way to save himself. He wrote about his situation and asked for help. It worked, naturally. On pretense, he showed up for the prosecution's case, and a few days later, he was freed. He instantly melted across the border without leaving a trace.

He had bad luck when he returned to Portugal many years later. That was his downfall. As an example of the principle that no one mind is always greater than all others, there was another man in the same line who was a more clever businessman. Having agreed with Argentino on a profitable shipment to Brazil, he executed the operation, put the profit in his pocket and never met with Argentino to finalize the deal.

A poor calculation.

Argentino tracked his partner down, carrying his Colt, and finished the story. This homicide, revealing the kind of man he was, in the end was simply a single act of bad judgment in a twenty-years-long chain of other crimes.

Although sentenced so heavily that he would already be quite old when he left prison, he nevertheless gave off few signs of being worried about it. To the contrary. He spoke with Catalan and the Captain as if he had the rest of his life waiting for him on the outside. He had his reasons. He had not forgotten the ministers and other VIPs who owed him juicy debts to pay for his silence about orgies and scandals. Surely those people had also not forgotten him. Life had taught him many times over that to procure silence, some people will do everything and more.

The Cat's Impossible Feat

Prisoners rarely spoke about escape. The general opinion was that no escape from there was possible. The prison administration, it was known, had taken past experience into account: the improbable attempt at escaping through the sewer pipes; 402's audacious jumping venture eight years before; and others, smothered at birth. Prison Services had a series of grates riveted into the pipes going in all directions. They ordered traps built where fugitives would drown in the slime had they succeeded in cutting the grates. They ordered the sealing of all access, installing barbed wire on the roofs of the storerooms, electrifying the fences and reinforcing the watchtowers both on top of the walls and on the outside.

402 laughed about it all. Talking with the Cat, he repeated what he'd always told Augusto whenever he'd run into him: "There's not a prison in the world from which there's no escape. If I were young and didn't have this damned leg, I wouldn't be here. You have a head and you have legs. If you think, you'll find a way."

The Cat didn't comment. He just gave 402's shoulder a friendly clap.

"I see you're going to be thinking," 402 said in a fatherly manner. The Cat thought.

He thought with such wisdom that he achieved what until then no one had done. Who knows by what means of communication, but by the following morning everyone in the prison had heard the news. Right away, too, people told various versions. When all is said and done, although many of the details never became clear, one idea remained as a historical truth: Cat had chosen for his final exit point the place and the manner that had appeared out of the question, not just for being the most difficult imaginable, but for being deemed most emphatically impossible.

He had been commissioned with repairing the deteriorated clerestory windows on the central tower and the roof on one of the wings. It was arduous work which involved metal cutting and soldering. There was no one other than the Cat who could complete it. He labored on it for weeks, walking the rooftop and clambering up the tower with the help of a long ladder he hoisted up for the job.

Up to that point, it was all clear. Afterward, it was a mystery: how he managed to leave his cell by night and reach the roof of the wing;

how he, by himself, could lift the ladder up to the wing roof and descend on it to the lowest roof of the administration buildings. The rest of the story gave even more cause for amazement. Right in front of the prison entrance, the administration buildings were separated from the guards' buildings, which faced onto the outside, by an inner roadway some four meters wide. Watchmen constantly surveilled that area. The Cat placed the ladder from roof to roof precisely above and a short distance from the watchman. From there, he walked across the road and then jumped over the outer wall to land just a few meters away from the watchman at the main door to the prison, right near where, years earlier, 402 had smashed his leg. There was no question about it: The ladder remained in place as if to mock the security system.

The director couldn't believe it. He inspected, investigated, examined and revisited the positioning of the ladder, but wasn't convinced.

"No, it didn't happen that way, it wasn't possible."

Years went by, and prisoners said the director continued pondering it, trying to uncover how the Cat actually managed to escape from prison.

Prisoners talked and laughed. Truth be told, they, too, could never understand how the Cat achieved such a feat.

A Change of Mess

Virgolino was the only person seeing the Communist isolated in a cell high up on the third-floor balcony of C Wing, when he delivered his mess tray. He didn't care to talk about it. He had express instructions to say nothing, and he complied, with one exception. He talked with Parrana because he trusted him. It was Parrana who told him about the PIDE, when they had brought the three Communists there years before. In any case, the last of the three Communists remained in isolation up on the third-floor balcony and received nothing from the outside.

Parrana thought and thought, and spoke to Virgolino. "The man must be sick of what you bring him after all these years. If you were to put something else on his mess tray from time to time, I would give some of my food."

"Don't even think about it!" Virgolino reacted. "The guard sees everything, and I don't want trouble."

Parrana continued to think, and gradually Virgolino started thinking, too. It took him more than a month to make up his mind, but he finally decided to do it.

So, for once, Virgolino exchanged the mess meant for the third-balcony man in solitary for the cod and potatoes that Parrana offered. Just once. It went well. Afterward, both of them found themselves comfortable with having run the risk, and they felt so natural about their action that every so often they repeated it.

A few days later, Sunday, heading to mass and already inside the chapel, Garino placed himself alongside Virgolino. Before mass began, just as Augusto used to ask Parrana, he whispered, "So, the man is still there?"

Virgolino nodded in the affirmative.

"He's still incommunicado?"

Virgolino confirmed it with another nod.

Garino couldn't contain himself: "Damn, that's got to stop!" He spoke a little louder than he intended.

"Shhhh," sacristan 333 warned from afar.

333 tried to stop anyone from taking advantage of mass to meet up or discuss plans or business. Maybe it's not correct to say he "tried." He pretended to try as a show in front of the priest and guards. Actually, he couldn't care less.

The Death of Old Lady-Killer

Serpentina had a new attack one evening and was taken to an infirmary cell still convulsing, biting his tongue and foaming. The crisis passed and, still in a state of some disorientation, he was leaning against the doorjamb to his cell distractedly watching the corridor. Suddenly, a group of aides burst through carrying a litter with another prisoner who had fainted. At a guard's direction, they disappeared into a neighboring cell. Serpentina recognized Old Lady-Killer. One of the aides leaving the cell said to the others, "This guy is finished."

Daytime, the infirmary cell doors remained open, and the guards' vigilance was not tight. The less sick stood at their cell doorways and sometimes conversed with the others. When Serpentina saw that the moment was right, he took three steps to look into the next cell.

It was, in fact, Old Lady-Killer. They had him in bed, on his back, the blanket all the way up to his nose. He wasn't moving and his eyes were closed. His breathing was quick and labored.

"Old Lady-Killer," Serpentina whispered.

He didn't respond.

"Old Lady-Killer," he repeated.

Nothing.

Serpentina withdrew and returned later.

This time, Old Lady-Killer gave off signs of life. He opened his eyes, then closed them again.

"How do you feel?" Serpentina asked.

Old Lady-Killer breathed deeply, and his words came out slowly and faintly.

"I'm bad, buddy. I'm not going to make it—"

"Don't say that!" Serpentina cut him off, and the figure of three hundred *contos* jumped into his mind. "You're gonna get better and carry on—"

"I'm bad," Old Lady-Killer repeated. "Not going to make it."

Silent a few minutes, Serpentina took up the conversation again. "You really think you're going to die?"

Old Lady-Killer nodded yes. There was no question he was pretty far gone.

Serpentina left, but returned after a while.

"Listen, Old Lady-Killer," and he placed his hand gently on the man's shoulder. "You know you can trust me. Tell me where you have the money buried so when I get out, I can turn it over to your kids."

Old Lady-Killer's sighed, "I have no kids."

"Well, I'll give it to your girlfriend—" Serpentina suggested.

"No girlfriend—"

"Hey, I didn't make it up. It was you who told me about it."

Old Lady-Killer didn't answer right away. Then he opened his eyes and in a weak but aggressive tone said, "Forget about it, guy! You're going before me."

In the end, Old Lady-Killer went before Serpentina, who told Silvino about his last conversation with him. "It's not right," he protested indignantly. "The guy died and took his dough with him."

Silvino was a tactful man who knew something about life.

"It's you that he took with him, Serpentina. The guy never had any buried money. He didn't have a cent. If he kept telling that story, it was to make himself feel good. What would we guys have thought of him if he had killed the old lady and gotten nothing out of it? He himself wound up believing the story he invented, and you know what? His years in prison were much easier for it."

A Woman in the Window

The infirmary arcade was the only place from which, over the roof-tops, the storerooms, the walls and the guard stations, you could see city residences on the other side of the street, some hundred or more meters away. The funnel-shaped asphalt triangles between the six wings of the star and the surrounding arc of workshop buildings had only the sky as horizon beyond the prison. The infirmary arcade was an opening to the exterior, the seductive vision of free space.

The windows you could see from there remained almost always shut however. When open, no one appeared in them, certainly because it had to be painful for the inhabitants of those upper-story apartments to see the sad spectacle of the prison's inside. Or because the women did not want to be subjected to any provocative or obscene gesture on the part of the prisoners. They must have been informed by experience.

There was one exception though. In one of those windows, alone among dozens of others, a woman appeared whenever the prisoners were walking in the arcade. She propped herself on the windowsill and stayed there, often until the prisoners went back to their cells. Distance did not allow her features to be discerned, but she appeared to be full-figured, with abundant black hair. She also could be seen looking down toward the street or across to the prisoners.

That woman could not possibly imagine the passions, the illusions and dreams that her far-off apparition provoked. It would have been difficult for the ordinary mortal to conjecture how far those feelings, attitudes and fantasies might lead. At times, you might say they were crazy. In fact, for the most part, they weren't. And if you could pen-etrate into the heart of the majority of those who walked by there, it would be the rare man whose eye was not irresistibly drawn to and fixed on that indistinct figure of the woman in the window.

Absurd though it may seem, Porto Alto, a level-headed man con-demned by mere fate for rioting at a bull run, convinced himself that she came to the window to see him, that he was the one she was look-ing at. His imagination soared so high that, even though it was impos-sible to distinguish her features, he had them all detailed in his mind. On an enormous sheet of thick paper that he somehow got hold of, he wrote in big letters: "I AM JOSÉ PINTO. WRITE TO ME AT NUMBER 225." And as his cell gave onto the arcade, he climbed up to his high little window and without knowing if she was still at her window, extended his arms through the grate and displayed his announce-ment for her to see. He did it so many times that the guards caught him and transferred him from his infirmary cell to one on the wings.

"I know she saw it," he told Benjamim confidentially before being transferred. "Any day her letter will come."

Nero was another. When he was in the infirmary, he also convinced himself that he was the one she was looking at. On the arcade, from one end to the other, he puffed out his substantial torso to stand out even more. Walking back and forth, he stepped quickly when he had his back toward the houses, and when he was facing the houses, he paraded by, deliberate and imposing, his eyes trained on the distant window. He sought to call her attention, he wanted her to see him and be impressed. And he believed he did so. Who knows how he came to believe it, but he was certain—more than certain!—it was Nero she was watching. Who could have predicted Nero's behavior? He, the giant, terror to guards and prisoners alike, did a somersault on the floor, yanked the cap from his head, and after a round of deep belly laughs, rubbed his hand repeatedly over his clean-shaven scalp.

"Ay, Holy Mary, Mother of God! It was her, dammit!"

Falua, who had observed everything, stopped to enjoy the scene. But Silvino, who was again in the infirmary, approached him and warned, "Be careful, son. Pretend you didn't see anything."

With 104, the issue could have turned more serious. When he went to the arcade, he always took special care to dress well, as if going to a party. On the outside, he went to a lot of fairs because his specialty was phony card games and other underhanded business. There wasn't a fairground where he didn't frequent the bordello, and he honestly believed the girls liked him. Now, here in the infirmary garden, watching the woman in the window, he couldn't keep from courting her—from a distance, clearly. He had to play all his trump cards. One thing he paid special attention to was his footwear. He put on snazzy socks with colored stripes. He seated himself on the edge of a wall turned toward the buildings, his leg extended, pulling his pant leg up to show off his sock. No, not for others to see. This was for her, no question about it, for her!

(By the way, reader, this really happened, it's not some made-up, imaginary story.)

This time, too, Falua enjoyed the show and started to laugh, and 104 did not like it. Gonçalo found him near the little garden shed, where 104 was sharpening a blade on a stone, a tense and strained look in his eyes. As he sharpened the blade, he looked across at the one who had mocked him.

"So, my friend," Gonçalo shot at him in his meek voice, "It's a beautiful day." And he kept standing there alongside, still and silent.

104 got the reason why Gonçalo stayed close by, and muttered a curse word. For a second, the temptation seized him to stick the blade

into Gonçalo's gut. If it was someone else, he might have done it. Without even knowing why, he felt it impossible to do it to Gonçalo, who remained just a couple of steps away, defenseless, as if he were paying him no mind, distractedly watching the arcade. Before long, 104 realized clearly that Gonçalo had appeared precisely to prevent him from doing anything really stupid.

A few more times, he passed the blade across the stone. Then, in a sudden move, he stopped.

The guard Ernesto, who was on duty at the infirmary, noticed there was something in the air. Falua with his malicious smile. Some of the others watching him. Imperceptible exchanges of glances. The prisoners' uncertain pacing back and forth on the arcade. And suddenly, without explanation, 104 coming out of hiding in the garden shed and Gonçalo appearing right after him.

Recreation in the arcade was going to end soon, but Ernesto thought it better not to wait. He blew his whistle and ordered the prisoners to line up.

"The bastard stole ten minutes from us!" a voice rose in protest.

What few knew was that on that day, a serious incident—which the woman in the window would never have guessed she was the cause of—was averted.

An Inexhaustible Subject

That day the conversation in Rolim's group revolved around the rude rejoinders posed by the young man who had come from Monsanto. Lately, it seemed he wanted to show he knew no less than the master.

"You talk, talk, talk, but it's all crap. Women might be very different like you say, but they all have the same hole, so they're all identical."

"That's your mistake," Rolim calmly pronounced. "If there are differences among women, perhaps the greatest difference is precisely the genitals."

"Genitals, genitals, genitals! Call it by its name, man," the young man retorted, at which he spouted off three or four crude synonyms.

"Different in form," Rolim continued, "different in size, different in the pattern of the hair, different in the facility for orgasm, different because for some it's pleasurable and for others it's painful, and different because some want to start right at the finish and others start but wind up declining."

"They say no, no, but they're lying," the other man interrupted.

"Wrong again," Rolim corrected him firmly. "When a woman says no, it can mean two different things. It could be protest, anger or a refusal, and it could be exactly the opposite: a tease, or the overly excited expectation of pleasure that she fears could be so intense."

"How do you tell the difference between one no and the other?" asked one of the listeners timidly.

"That's a vitally important question," Rolim explained. "If you don't know how to distinguish, you run two risks. If you reject her refusal, it's like you're violating her. Or you have compassion for her and retreat as though you don't have the energy for it precisely when she most desires you."

"Then how do you tell the difference?" the man from Monsanto insisted.

Rolim stalled. Uncharacteristically, nothing came out in response. Always so sure of himself, this time the expression on that small face dominated by the hat with the big numbers 444 exposed his insecurity. The guard's lineup whistle rescued him.

One of those present recalled Nero's laughter and comment from long ago: "Listening to you, you sound like a professor, but looking at you, you look like a charlatan."

In the middle of the conversation, Argentino stopped to listen. Tall, serene, visibly apart from the others, but obviously amidst them, with his vacant face, he listened without reaction, then moved along.

Serpentina, who also stopped by the group just as Rolim's weakness had been exposed, couldn't take his eyes off Argentino. When Argentino walked away, Serpentina became annoyed.

"Fucking crazy," he muttered to himself. "I don't get that guy. He probably knows more than Rolim, but he don't say nothing."

Tony's Tabes Dorsalis

It was the second case of *tabes dorsalis*. At least, so the nurse said. Since no one knew any other name for the disease, everyone repeated it. Some people had heard the doctor say it was syphilis. As the nurse had higher authority, the disease kept being referred to by what he said. In the first case, 309's progress was slow. He began getting depressed and then started walking hunched over and stumbling. He started talking less and less, and finally not at all. Now, bent over almost at a right angle, dragging his feet and slobbering on himself, he couldn't control either urine or feces. Soon, there seemed to be little of a human being left. It was something alive, but without intelligence or feeling. To the surprise of a casual observer, the aides treated him patiently, undressing him, bathing him and tidying him up the best they could.

Now Tony was the second case. The progress of the disease was rapid, maybe not even a week. It was almost instantaneous. In a few days, his condition became literally the same as 309's. But not the same was the treatment he received from the aides. They showed impatience with him and at times left him in his cell in the midst of his filth.

"All I needed was another case like this," Benjamim grumbled when he saw Tony in that state. "Let him stew in his shit for all I care."

He certainly did stew.

Some time after, there was a shakeup. New prisoners arrived, others were transferred. Tony and one other got out on conditional release. The other guy's release didn't raise any comment, but Tony's received a lot.

"To let that wretched guy go? For what?" Benjamim questioned. "So he can wind up in the gutter?"

Tony, a guard explained, had someone who cared for him and had promised Prison Services they'd take him in.

"Do you believe it?" Benjamim asked Augusto the gardener. "I don't. I don't believe anyone would want that shit in their house."

Friends

Silvino frequently talked with Augusto the gardener on the infirmary arcade. They talked about life and the world. Talking with Augusto, Silvino didn't ramble on, as he did with Serpentina, about the origin of species, time and space. Their conversation was more intimate and affectionate.

Over the course of years, they had become friends. Each of their lives was quite different, as were the crimes that led them there. Silvino, at the margins of society since his helter-skelter boyhood without any help or recourse, almost fatalistically followed the path of single-handedly grabbing what he needed to survive. He lived like that until taken prisoner the last time, already in his forties. From childhood, Augusto had enjoyed the normal life, hard but peaceful, of a highland family of poor farmers.

What brought them together and gave them pleasure when they met and talked were their similar ways of thinking and their feelings about things. They'd never spoken about their respective sentences, nor what led to them. It's as if all that was alien matter that had nothing to do with their situation or their interests now. That day, though, who knows by what association of ideas, Augusto posed a curious question.

"Listen, Silvino. If one day you were to break into a door and enter a house without knowing who owned it, and once inside you saw, by the photographs you found, that it was me who lived there, what would you do? Would you still steal whatever was there?"

Unusually for him, Silvino smiled, and his answer came quickly. "You judge me harshly, Augusto," he said. "If that happened, I would be so ashamed I would put everything down and wish I were a hundred kilometers away."

Augusto, always with a serious face, smiled too.

Certainly, absolutely certainly, Silvino was telling the truth.

Impunity for Wild Boar, Number 509

509 approached and asked for a light, Serpentina handed him his lighter, and 509 lit his cigarette. Then, when Serpentina held out his hand to get the lighter back, 509 casually dropped it in his pocket as though he were its rightful owner and calmly kept walking on his way.

Serpentina started to go after him for it, but Silvino grabbed his arm. "Don't mess with him or it'll end badly for you."

"It's my lighter!" said a stunned Serpentina.

"It was," Silvino said. "Now it's his."

Serpentina wouldn't hear of it. He ran up alongside 509, who stood there tense, looking in fact like a wild boar ready to lurch.

"The lighter?!" Serpentina demanded.

"Ah, the lighter!" 509 exclaimed. He pulled it out of his pocket and handed it over without a further word.

A euphoric Serpentina returned to Silvino. "So, in the end he's not as ferocious as you say. He gave it to me!"

"Don't believe it," Silvino answered. "You'll pay for this, and dearly."

509 was one of thirty prisoners invited to attend the communal hall created by the new director. It was one of the few reforms that hadn't been wiped out. It's hard to understand what led them to choose 509 because the hall had been announced as their own place for prisoners in rehabilitation. 509 had never been punished, nor was he ever caught: There was never any proof. Still, everyone knew about his more or less serious misdeeds of which the other prisoners were victim.

"We're being duped," said one of the chosen when he saw 509 among the thirty. "That guy is going to make our lives miserable."

And so he did.

The guards proceeded with the morning count-off in the hall and noticed one prisoner missing. It wan't hard to find him.

Wrapped in his blanket, Serpentina lay in his bed facedown and unconscious. They couldn't miss seeing the blood pooled on his undershirt. More guards came, and they called aides to carry him to an infirmary cell.

Treated for two blows on his back, he recovered after a few weeks. No one investigated or determined who had committed the aggression. Nor was the weapon found after a thorough search. Remembering the incident with the lighter a few days before, everybody believed it was 509, Wild Boar. By deduction, just about everyone knew it was 509. But no one mentioned either his number or his name. He, along with everyone else in the hall, was called before the head guard, who asked if they had witnessed anything. No one had seen anything.

"I was sleeping," answered 509, like many others.

The case was closed. No one gave it further importance.

Visitors for Catalan and the Captain

Two chic young women, accompanied by a guard, walked delicately that day through the corridor that led to a room meant for certain private visits.

"There go the Captain's little girlfriends," remarked Falua, who happened to see them.

Girlfriends they weren't. And only one was the Captain's. The other was Catalan's.

These two visitations, in person and apart from the visiting booths, gave rise to envy as much as mockery. Envy, naturally, because all others had to receive their visitors in the booths, and besides which, the Captain and Catalan were both up in years and in sad shape, and the girls were bombshells. Mockery, because the men set themselves up for it.

The site designated for such visits was cold in summer and freezing in winter. That's how the scandal started. In the set-up where they would receive their special favors, the two interested parties had arranged that they would use nothing more nor less than two rubber hot water bottles. They were, rather uncommonly, purposed to protect the frozen knees of the poor girls. Aside from being unusual, this might have passed unnoticed. The worst part is that at the end of the visit, before they returned to their cells, the Captain and Catalan went to the door to spill the still steaming water from the rubber bottles down the drain.

Those who beheld that scene died laughing.

"So, my child, was the Captain's water nice and warm?"

"Hey, old-timer! Why don't you put the rubber in your pants to fill out what you don't got?"

Catalan and the Captain knew there was such talk and were furious inside, but pretended not to hear.

A Hard Winter

That day, as on many other days, sometimes for weeks on end, there was no recreation. The rain battered the immense, colorless walls of the six wings laid out in a star. Beneath the rain, enveloped in an ashy fog, the huge building looked like something dead: looked like, but inside, hundreds of lives dragged on. Inside those walls, the obligatory ritual functions repeated themselves day after day. Whistles, noises, sounds, movements, smells, lineups, count-offs—with one difference: Except for the hundred or so employed in the workshops and internal workings of the prison, the other four hundred spent the whole time locked in their cells. Locked up and alone.

People naturally had different reactions. Some had authorized pastimes making belts knot by knot or string bags. Others spent their days endlessly pacing back and forth like penned animals. Others recalled the deeds that landed them there. Others made plans for their future, even if that future would begin only after ten, fifteen or twenty years when they'd completed their prison sentences. Others wrapped themselves in erotic fantasies. Others lay down and slept or pretended to. Others almost hibernated, unable to think about anything at all. And still others, having lost their sense of time, which seemed interminable, remained attuned to all sounds, always waiting for the moment to receive their mess or to count off, or for the door to open, breaking the isolation and solitude. Then they would look out, toward the immensity of the wing that was as solemn as a cathedral nave, and feel an illusory whiff of space, amplitude, atmosphere and freedom.

A well-known author, so it was told, asked the prison, and was given authorization to stay locked up in a cell for twenty-four hours. He explained that he was writing a novel, and he had a character in it who was doing hard time. The author wanted to have first-hand experience of how a man sentenced to fifteen years of maximum security prison would feel being locked in a cell for so many years. One day, of course, is not the same as fifteen years or, counting leap years, five thousand four hundred seventy-eight days. But the author considered his experience sufficient.

It's not known if the novel, once written and published, was ever sent to the penitentiary library. Therefore, it's not known if any prisoner had a chance to read it. It would be interesting to hear their opinions.

Assaults in the Sintra Mountains

Except in a few especially trusted cases, the admission of newspapers and possession of a radio were unauthorized. The prisoners knew very little of what was happening on the outside. Important news of the world, and even of the country, either never arrived or arrived late, sometimes years late. With one exception. Particularly serious crimes, prison terms and sentences became known right away, and spread around with greater detail than the newspapers printed.

It seemed a mystery how such news arrived. Visits took place in the booths with thick panes of glass and under strict guard watch. Correspondence was opened, carefully read by so-called "social assistants," and delivered after being censored and rubber stamped. Presents that family brought for the prisoners were controlled and searched. In the workshops, strict vigilance intercepted conversations between prisoners and people who came in from the outside.

That left the guards. In principle, they should have been the most zealous to comply with the established rules but, surprising though it may sound, the common thinking was that they were the first ones to give the prisoners such news.

In that regard, 402 had his own opinion. "If unauthorized money comes in, if pornographic magazines come in, if hashish comes in, why shouldn't such news come in?"

There was one news story that because of its nature captured the prisoners' imagination for many weeks.

There was a series of armed assaults in the mountains around Sintra. Malveira da Serra, Lagoa Azul, Capuchos, on the Pena and Penedo roads, São Pedro, all throughout the region. Cars on the highways fell prey to ambushes, and a masked man holding a gun cleaned out the passengers.

The assailant wasn't caught, and stories started to circulate. One time, finding some poor guy with absolutely nothing in his empty pockets, the masked man handed him a couple of sizable banknotes. In another case, the driver having fainted from shock, the assailant took control of the steering wheel and drove the car to the outskirts of town. In another instance, coming face to face with a well-known local strongman accompanied by two beauties, he forced the man to get out of his car and remove his pants, and he drove the car several kilometers away. Aside from these pranks, it was clear that from his dozens of assaults, the masked man had to have stolen a very large amount of moolah.

Months passed; they organized search posses and laid in wait for the assailant. Now pausing for a long break, now making a surprise attack, the masked man continued as lord of the land.

In the penitentiary, the story passed with admiration from one to another in the most inventive versions. Except for those whose interest or enthusiasm couldn't be stirred for anything in the world, the Sintra Mountains assaults turned into something like a modern chivalry romance.

A Sad End to the Passion of Nazaré

The news exploded like a bomb. In a few days, the whole penitentiary heard it. 31 had led Nazaré on. The address he had given him years before, supposedly of his sister who visited him, was in fact a bordello where his friend Ivette lived and with whom he schemed up the hoax. Nazaré's letters were read by the girls, who together dictated or wrote the responses. Not all of them felt the same way. Some laughed, others cried. Some wanted to put erotic and even obscene suggestions in the letters, others offered words corresponding to their own feelings evoked by each one of Nazaré's sentiments.

Ivette, 31's girlfriend, came up with the main idea: "You can see the guy deserves some sympathy. Let's have fun with him, but we don't have to hurt him."

And so, except for slight lapses, the letters to Nazaré were always authentic love letters, even sincere.

Reaction in the penitentiary was diverse. A few rare voices rose up to protest the abuse, but generally, the repercussion was otherwise. In a word: cruel. 31 even gained a certain respect in the others' eyes as anyone would who pulled off a big scam, Nazaré coming out like a fool worthy of ridicule.

Insulting words rained on him:

"Hey, Nazaré! When's the wedding?" "Hey, Nazaré! Aren't I invited to the ceremony?"

They shouted out to him as he passed. They yelled from morning's light to evening lockdown, through the tiny windows that gave onto the vast open spaces at recreation. They wouldn't let up.

Nazaré never talked with anyone about how he felt. He never asked 31 for an explanation. He just stopped talking to him. He also stopped attending visiting day for many months without a word to his mother. And for long months, he stopped going to recreation to save himself from his companions' wisecracks.

Almost a year later, on opening the door of his cell, they found him hanging from a belt attached up on the window bars.

"It's already five this year," said Benjamim, summoned with others to carry the body away.

"That won't be all," Silvino quietly pronounced when he heard what happened.

How Viseu Was Convicted

Out in the country, the case of Viseu was a mystery to the investigators for quite some time. The body had been found in a deserted field on the outskirts of town, fatally shot point-blank in two places, the head and the chest. No one heard the shots. No one saw any meeting, argument or conflict with the victim, a guy with a bad reputation in the area. The police came, went to the crime site, proceeded with their routine inspections, listened to family members and various others, but couldn't finger any suspect.

They spoke of two avenues of pursuit. One was the bullets themselves. When the police sought to find out who possessed arms, only two townspeople presented their hunting rifles, and the grocer ran to show them his pistol. The shots did not come from a hunting rifle, and the bullets from the pistol did not match the crime weapon. The other avenue was a cigarette lighter that a policeman claimed he found near the body, but that he had not shown to anyone.

Weeks passed and people concluded that the killer must not have been from the area. Most believed he would never be found. But one day, an agent reappeared in the tavern, showing the lighter of a peculiar shade of yellow, and asked if anyone knew who owned it.

From that point, events sped up. Crawling as well as he could, Viseu went to the town and was arrested. He confessed to being the owner of the lighter and described it in such a way as to leave no doubt. The next day, he led the police to a deserted, distant place and showed where he had buried the weapon. He was tongue-tied, his voice barely audible, but his confession was clear and the evidence was beyond question.

Viseu did not explain a reason for his act. Maybe he didn't even know it himself.

The police sought out his family—a brother and his wife and a bunch of children. Appearing thunderstruck by the events, they only gave confusing statements.

Looking at Viseu, seeing him hobbling lamely with a bum leg, his arms afflicted by hookworms and difficult to move, seeing his contorted mouth, the agents had trouble believing him.

"Why did you want a pistol?" asked one.

He gave no explanation, but simply shrugged his shoulders.

"Confound it!" another remarked. "How did you even manage to fire point-blank so perfectly?"

"Yes, it's hard to explain," commented a third. "He doesn't even know how he did it."

The court did not share that view. They sentenced Viseu to eight years in maximum security prison followed by twelve of banishment, exchangeable for eighteen years in prison.

In prison, Viseu never complained. He seemed to adapt. Surprisingly, he showed a sunny disposition in the way he expressed himself, in his gestures and in his quick responses to whatever they ordered him to do.

Every few months, his visitors gave him tremendous happiness. His brother, sister-in-law, nieces and nephews came, spoiling him with presents. And they said their goodbyes with unmistakably loving gestures.

Conditional Release

For some, conditional release was their only hope; for others, a dream or plan. It neither fell from the sky nor came by spontaneous decision by some judge. You had to conquer it, and to do so you had no better routes than the good graces of important protectors or repentance before God. Not by prayers in private, but by persistence in showing off.

There were exceptions. On Wing C, Old Man loudly appealed for forgiveness for his sins every day. He was too sincere and poor to be pardoned. Others who knew the world better had reason to hope and act. In one wing, and later in the infirmary cell where he was placed on a permanent basis not for being sick but because he was a doctor and protected, the rapist of anesthetized patients spent hours on his knees so that the guards peering through the peephole could see him posturing. Little Friar, the sacristy rat always with his hands together, forever paraded the religiosity he acquired during his years spent in the seminary. 333, who claimed to have murdered his two partners to defend his honor, was the devoted sacristan in service to the chapel. Any one of these had their prize almost guaranteed.

These were good examples to follow. Every Sunday, almost like a great worm ascending and descending the circular staircase that led up the rotunda to the chapel and to the confessional, a regular stream of repentants retold or reinvented their crimes, beating their breasts with their hands, and asking the priest not only for indulgences but also for a recommendation to Prison Services for conditional release or a pardon to shorten their sentences.

Judging by the results, and by what people said, from time to time God listened to those who called on him. You could truly believe in divine intervention. Because if not for God's hand, it would be hard to comprehend how, in those cases, the prison administration and Prison Services would facilitate their release. Any other criteria would advise against it to prevent recidivism.

Little Friar left prison four years before completing his term. He had been sentenced for rape and homicide under suspicion of having mutilated his victim's corpse. He confessed to the rape, but not the homicide. The victim disappeared, true, but nothing against Little Friar was proved. Now released, everyone swore he would never mess up again. Within a few months, the newspapers carried the story: Little Friar tried to rape a woman, but she escaped, threw herself into a river, shouted, was rescued, and then denounced him. With this new crime, unproved suspicions about his first crime came back. Rigorous investigation did the rest. Little Friar confessed to having killed and buried the first victim. The police went to dig up the site he had indicated—and discovered her remains.

Day by day, the authorities' unscrupulous incompetence and irresponsibility in evaluating each man's personality lengthened their catalogue of mistakes in observation, knowledge and decision, around the question of conditional release and other subjects.

That's how it was, too, when the shocking news quickly spread to everyone in the penitentiary: Tony was not sick—not with the famous *tabes dorsalis* nor with anything else. It was all deception. He played the part so well that he fooled everyone.

"So, boys," Benjamim said, "the guy took us all in for sure. No doubt about it, he was an artist."

The bad part is that once on the loose, Tony reverted to type. The police already attributed new crimes of the same nature to him: violently yanking the earrings off the women he raped. He hadn't been captured yet, but the papers were already sure he was the culprit.

"Now it's this one, but there'll be more to come," Garino said to Augusto.

Playing the system worked. Argentino, the Captain and Catalan, among others, spoke as though conditional release was within sight. The doctor, however—the rapist of anesthetized women—didn't trust anyone enough to say anything out loud. But you have to take it as a given that if he did not have protection and promises, he would never have continued his whole act of ostentatious prayer.

Silvino's Further Reflections

Quick-minded and curious, Serpentina liked listening to Silvino. What he had said about the common origin of the whole animal kingdom stayed in his memory, and in his doubts. One day, he returned to the topic.

"What you said—were you joking or for real?" he asked.

"If I was joking, I wouldn't have said it. And I'll add more. You can see a lot of plants with organs and life systems hardly different from animals. Even reproduction. There's male and there's female. Pollen, that yellow powder, just like sperm in a man, monkey, dog or cat, fertilizes the feminine sex in flowers."

Serpentina laughed. "Hey, man, don't exaggerate."

"Exaggerate? Why? Because a plant doesn't have nerves and a brain? It stands to reason. If an apple had nerves and a brain, I wouldn't want to hurt it by biting into it."

Silvino delivered his words with such conviction that Serpentina lost his impulse to laugh.

"Maybe," he said incredulously.

The two of them were now in infirmary cells, so they spent their recreation conversing.

Prodded by Serpentina's questions, Silvino further elaborated the breadth of his reflections.

Serpentina doubted it all from the start, though also experienced the thrill of profound excitement. He returned to his cell and couldn't get it out of his head. He was already convinced that humans descended from the ape, but he found Silvino's theory that all animals had a common origin absurd, and doubted even more so what he said about plants. He thought, and thought some more, but the suspicions kept growing. Aside from which, how about the time it must necessarily have taken for such extraordinary evolution and change?

Silvino had a ready answer to that question.

"The scientists say the earth was formed many millions of years ago. That's not much. To my mind, the day will come when science reaches the conclusion that those numbers are mistaken, and the evolution of living beings lasted ten or a hundred times longer than the time they estimated until now."

He said this with the same simplicity and assurance with which he had earlier, in the infirmary garden, explained the life of spiders and the African ant.

Silvino also had certain ideas about space. When he discoursed about that, Serpentina, despite his fertile imagination, had even more difficulty following him.

"I've been thinking," Silvino said, "that the infinite is an invention of man precisely because man cannot imagine it. I've also been thinking that the universe could be circular and that straight lines are curves."

Although he noticed Serpentina's shock, he continued without a pause. "I'm thinking that if you could walk always to the right, always, always, always, for centuries and centuries always to the right, you'd end up coming back to the same place."

And on another thread: "You look out at space and you ask yourself, how does it end? Where does it end? You look at a fly and you say, This is only what it is, it's practically nothing, it ends here. I've thought a lot and I think that's wrong. The world that's inside the tiniest being is as immense as the world outside. First, because the more you divide, there'll always be more you can divide, and second, the more you add, there'll always be more you can add."

That day, Augusto the gardener was around, watering and tending the plants. A disturbed Serpentina left Silvino and went over to Augusto. "Yo, man, I never guessed. Silvino's a decent fellow, I like him, he knows a lot, he's smart, but he's not well in the head. He's totally crazy with his theories."

Augusto knew them both well and tried to soothe him. "Don't worry. If his intelligence is working, it's because he's alive. If Silvino talks that way about space, it's because he has his feet firmly planted on the ground."

Serpentina was nearly shocked by that response. "So, you too?"

Augusto gave him a friendly cuff on the shoulder.

"Either I'm the crazy one or you two are," Serpentina summed up before he walked off. "It's okay if it's me."

The Electric Tram Man

A little group in one corner of the yard was engaged in animated conversation. Two of them were prison veterans. The others had just arrived a few days before, coming from a district jail.

"You see this guy here with the innocent face?" asked one veteran pointing to one of the recent men. "No doubt you've heard of him. He's the Electric Tram Man."

The indicated man told his story.

"This jerk fell like an innocent angel. I followed him from the station exit. Right away, I saw he was a yokel. He didn't know anything about Lisbon and he asked me for the Campo de Ourique. 'Hey, man,' I said to him, 'I'm going there myself, so let's go together.' We hopped onto an electric tram and, as usual, when I see the conductor, I bought a ticket for him and I showed my pass. From the shocked look on this idiot's face, I figured: *You're going to fall, there's no saving you now.* Before he could ask me anything, I said to him, 'You know what, my friend? This is a good business!' The moron looked at me bug-eyed with his mouth open and asked, 'Are you part of it?' 'Of course, I am,' I said, 'I'm a partner.' The rest was a piece of cake. The guy got all excited, we met up over the next few days taking a few more rides on the electric car so I could show off my pass. Two days later, I sold him an electric tram car."

His audience laughed hilariously and, the conversation over, they split and continued strolling.

"That guy is amazing!" marveled one of the newcomers who heard the story.

A veteran went up to him and destroyed the effect of the joke.

"Don't be taken in. It's a tall story. The man who sold an electric tram car died many years ago. It's an ancient tale. The guy who told it is here for another reason. He broke into so many doors and used his gun so much that he finally got caught."

Just then, as they were talking, the doctor in cell 8 of C Wing passed by with his customary pretentious airs. As always, he never spoke to anyone.

Wild Boar asked, "And what do you think of that piece of shit?"

"He's with you, my innocent angel!" another prisoner quipped, almost cutting off his way.

The doctor didn't look and pretended not to hear.

Generally speaking, no prisoner was completely excluded by the others from the community. Naturally, there were closer relationships and friendships, and also incompatible ones, conflicts and hatreds, but total exclusion only in rare cases. That was the case with Lizard, the one who gave his wife's liver to his children to eat. And it was the case with the supercilious doctor who anesthetized his patients in order to rape them, displayed contempt for all the other prisoners, and made a constant spectacle of prayer and repentance like a bad actor.

Gonçalo's Gesture

A Transmontano, like Augusto from the province of Trás-os-Montes in the northeast of the country, Gonçalo chatted with him whenever the opportunity arose. They had similar cases: Both were victims of grave and shocking injustice and were involved against their will in situations that led them to prison, not of their own fault but of others. There was a death in one case, a serious injury in the other. Society, or those who rule, turn from guilty to accusers. They who rule make the law and condemn.

"I made a point of coming to talk with you," Gonçalo said to Augusto that morning when they met. "I get out in a week and I remembered I wanted to share something with you."

He had thought about it a lot. The idea wouldn't go away. It had to do with the political prisoner in isolation on C Wing.

"You know very well how our mountains and villages are. No one would find him there. I'm leaving you my address. If you get to talk with him some day, tell him when he gets out to come find me, and he can live there however long he wants. We don't have much, but he won't lack for anything."

Augusto had a more realistic view of things. First, he didn't know if he'd ever get the chance to convey the offer. Second, it didn't seem to him that the man, if he were ever set free, would want to seek refuge in the mountains. Nevertheless, he didn't want to destroy Gonçalo's illusion.

"Don't worry. If I have the chance, I'll do what you ask."

Gonçalo got his freedom shortly afterward. He never knew if Augusto passed his message along or not. In any case, one presumes that for a long time up there in the mountain villages of Trás-os-Montes, he felt an inner contentment for having made the offer. Beyond that, he nurtured the hope that one day he would come knocking on his door—the unknown Communist isolated for long years on C Wing.

The Raviolis

"Look at them!" one prisoner said suddenly to another. The other looked.

A little group that had arrived just a few days before stood apart. The uniform, the cap, the numbers were all normal. But something else distinguished them. Still young, they looked more closely shaved and cleaner, as if they'd just been ironed. Besides, they all wore shoes. And freshly shined. With their serious, earnest faces, they all peered without talking in the same direction. At what, no one noticed.

"They're the Raviolis."

"Oh!"

No one knew where the name came from. Their case had been widely reported in the newspapers and was familiar in the prison: bank assaults with ladies' stockings to mask their faces, sawed-off shotguns, barrages of bullets, the death of a National Republican Guard, false documents, an innumerable collection of serious crimes.

It was the first time they appeared at recreation. Everyone looked their way. It appeared the three didn't look toward anyone.

The next day, someone asked them for a cigarette. One of the three pulled out a pack of Americans, gave him one, lit it for him with his lighter, then completely ignored him.

"See, they're decent types," said the smoker, drawing on his cigarette.

Silvino thought otherwise, but didn't say. He observed and decided for himself. In that studied comportment of men in the flower of life, in that arrogance, in those pampered and apparently serene, indifferent faces, he read cold determination and cruelty.

In time, the Raviolis evoked contradictory reactions: antipathy of some, idolatry from others. Always bathed and freshly shaved, in contrast to the general slovenliness, they didn't get involved, didn't create problems, didn't have a nasty word for anyone. Always the three of them together and to themselves, they were so obviously different from everyone else they seemed to have wound up there by mistake.

It was clear they were revolted by their companions, particularly those renowned for their brutishness and bravado, like Wild Boar and Nero. The contrast between these veteran crime heroes and the three bank robbers with their sawed-off shotguns was so patent it could not escape Garino's malicious observation.

"And here you have the modern generation, boys!" he said to those around him. "The future belongs to them."

The Employee's Question

After a series of transfers from one job to another, some two years ago Garino had been moved from aide in the A Wing to the cardboard workshop. He received the same pittance, but anyway the work was different and cleaner.

A new employee had recently joined the staff, a young man who came in every day from an industrial town in the suburbs. He had a calm way about him, without the customary repressive instincts. He got on well with the prisoners, and they got along well with him.

Outside of talk about work, he often drew closer to Garino to exchange a few private words, almost in secret, avoiding attention from the guards. Small observations, passing comments, that brought them together.

One time, in a casual encounter, Augusto asked Garino how things were in the workshop. Garino responded, referring to the latest novelty.

"There's a new employee now who's really nice."

At times, Garino was aware of slight hesitations in the employee, as if he wanted to say more than he was saying. That something more came out one day, when he spurted out, "Listen, aren't there some political prisoners here?"

For reasons difficult to explain, it was precisely the question that Garino had been expecting for a long time. If not that question, then at least the subject. In a few words, quietly so the guard wouldn't hear, he related what happened with the three Communists on the third balcony of C Wing, and how after all these years, there was still one who remained in complete isolation.

That was the end of the conversation. The employee didn't comment.

"That was something new," Garino told Augusto as he related what had occurred. "It's the first time anything like that happened to me. I told him what he wanted, but what else does the guy want?"

"Be careful," Augusto advised. "They have informers all over the place."

A Mystery Is Revealed

At long last, the whereabouts of the masked assailant in the Sintra Mountains was discovered in an isolated cottage near Lourel. Early one morning, the police surrounded the house in force, and someone knocked firmly on the door. Their reception was less common than usual in cases like these. From inside came a fusillade of bullets, and the surprised police retreated. After a few minutes, they attacked and invaded the house with guns firing, but the man was not there.

They launched a manhunt truly worthy of American films. They cut off streets and roads and managed to pick up the scent and follow his trail. They finally ambushed him near Telhal up in the bare, rugged Carregueira Mountains. It was no easy operation. Surrounded, the fugitive once again fired back at the police. He had a good aim, so the charge took some time. Between a shot here and a shot there, they spent the whole day without success.

As twilight set in, an anguished silence fell over the hills. It was hard for either hunter or prey to know what to do. Unaccustomed to situations like this, the police couldn't decide how to proceed. The shooting over, the fugitive disappeared.

Only at dusk did the case end. Unexpectedly emerging from behind some bushes, the fugitive risked a run for it. After five or ten meters a single bullet cut him down. After so many shots fired in vain, this one hit him right on target. The man died.

The case became known in the penitentiary, and overall, they lauded the valor of the masked man of the Sintra Mountains. If that's how they felt even without knowing his identity, the general admiration soon turned into veneration and legend. The masked man of the Sintra Mountains was none other than Cat, the talented Cat, who years earlier had pulled off the most spectacular prison escape ever known.

The Gray Kitten

Several prisoners gathered to watch the show—a young cat, soft gray, with watery green eyes, amazing poses and movements. In constant motion, it lay on its back gently rocking its body and waving its legs slowly and languorously, exposing its belly of glossy whitish fur. Then it gently rolled over onto itself as if stretching in slow motion. It mewed incessantly—a weak, pleasant meow, profound and loving.

The speechless men were riveted by the scene. Fixated, nothing could tear them away from the view. Some, their hands concealed in their pockets, caressed themselves as if the kitten were seducing them personally.

"Hey, boys!" one couldn't help but exclaim, "it looks like a woman!"

"It's obviously not," another corrected. "There are women who look like cats when they're in heat."

The spectacle ended when they heard the whistle. Recreation was over. They lined up in twos; the guards proceeded with the count and led them back to their cells in a sullen cortege.

A few days later, working in the garden, Augusto found the dead body of the gray cat against the wall. Coiled up, battered, stiff, blotted with already black blood. He figured someone had abused it brutally and then killed it. He decided not to say anything and buried it right there.

Ruminating hard about it later, he concluded it must have been another prisoner who worked in the garden who had been caught one other time with an animal. He was further convinced when he met him later that same day and saw still fresh scratches on his hands and face that the guy himself couldn't explain.

Augusto never told anyone. He understood that such things happened there and it was best to bury them like dead animals and not speak of them any further.

The Funky-Fish Revolt

The prison administration proceeded with its investigation. The head guard, the head officers on each wing, the social assistant and the director himself, all conducted lengthy interrogations of dozens of the confined men. They found nothing indicating that there had been a plan for the mutiny. As if to confirm the existence of a conspiracy, they randomly sent several men into solitary on bread and water. They discovered nothing, in all probability because there was nothing to discover.

Nevertheless, the causes for what happened were plain to see. Years and years on end, five years according to some, more than ten according to others, two or three times a week, the lunch was dried beans and funky-fish. The beans were okay if served only once in a while. The funky-fish, which they called it because no one recognized it as anything else, was positively indigestible. It smelled of old garbage and tasted of creolin soap. The prisoners rumored that the guard who ran the kitchen made a fortune on that dish.

The mutiny broke out at lunchtime, when the aides distributed the mess trays to the cells. Hearing shouting resonating throughout the naves of the wings, the guards on duty gave no importance to it at first. Then came the shock wave. The clamor took over the whole prison, mixed with the deafening pounding of trays against iron bars. In the face of such vigorous protest, the guards on the wings ran to close the cell doors with the ratchet of two turns of the locks and the jolt of safety bolts.

In a few minutes the situation worsened. Through the grated windows in the cells, a torrent of mess trays went flying down on the recreation yards below, spreading fish and beans everywhere. After the cleanup, the guards counted almost 300 trays. The more they sounded the shrieking alarm whistles, the more the uproar grew, uniting the whole penitentiary in one gigantic protest chorus.

Punished indiscriminately, Porto Alto, 31, Falua and several others were put in isolation cells in the basement. With the exception of Catalan, the Captain, 333, as well as Nero, Wild Boar and a few others generally exempt from punishment, all other prisoners were denied recreation and visitors for a month.

The dish in question did not get served for a whole year. Later, it returned, though less frequently.

A Surprising Conversation

Porto Alto went through a crazy period. He convinced himself that the woman in the window in the apartment across the street was looking straight at him. Not even he knew how such a thing was possible when he wrote his name in enormous letters on a big piece of paper that he dangled out his grated peephole window so the unknown woman would read it from afar and write to him. Craziness indeed; but it didn't last long. Apart from that, Porto Alto was a reasonable man.

That day, he received a visit from his wife. It was the usual kind of visit, calm, talking about current issues in life and in the future. But that day, he lost himself in the conversation.

He really did want to keep on paying attention to what his wife was saying. The more he tried, he couldn't. Little by little, the conversation in the next booth drew his attention away.

101 was there, and visiting him was his daughter. The prisoners discussed that visitor quite a bit because 101 had been sentenced for having raped his three daughters, and this was the only one who came to visit. It was said, and everything indicated it was true, that the others and the rest of his family had cut him off.

As much as he peered over to the next booth, Porto Alto couldn't see the girl's face through the grates and the double glass panes. But in compensation, and surprisingly, her voice came through clearly, sweet and steady.

"Yes, father. I'll bring what you're asking for. I'll work it out, don't worry. I can't take you out of here, but I can help you."

After a pause, "I see you're about to cry, father. Don't cry, because otherwise I'll start crying, too."

Another pause, and once again the girl's tender voice: "Have courage, okay?"

"You're not paying attention to anything I'm saying," Porto Alto's wife protested.

There was no time left for her to repeat it. The visit ended, and the guards conducted the prisoners back to their cells.

The Isolation Broken

Whenever occasion arose that allowed for conversations on the fly between Garino and the employee in the cardboard workshop, they became evermore personal. The employee gave him news of what was happening in the world and spoke of working-class struggles in his area. Garino remembered long-ago struggles of the workers in Alentejo. The reciprocal trust they developed led to the employee one day making an explosive request.

"Listen, wouldn't it be possible for me to give you a small thing to pass along to the comrade in isolation?"

Garino barely registered any surprise at the word "comrade." He'd never heard it used that way, but it seemed natural. One after another, several answers occurred to him in succession: It's impossible...it's almost impossible...it's not possible...it would be very difficult. But the reply that came out was, "I'll see!"

And he did. He had no contact with people on C Wing, so he had to find another way. From him to Augusto, from Augusto to Virgolino. As for himself, he felt up to the risk. Now he needed to get the others on board.

It took more than a month to suss out the possibility. Right away Augusto declared himself ready to help, as if he had been waiting for an opportunity like this for a long time. Virgolino was a harder sell. At first, he said no. Then that he'd think about it. Finally, he asked a specific question: "Pass along what? If it's a weapon, forget it."

No, no way was it a weapon. The employee from the suburbs clarified to Garino that it was only a matter of a small piece of blue soap, exactly the same as the prison provided the inmates. Smaller even than a bar of soap. Garino, Augusto and Virgolino found that weird, but they understood what was involved and all agreed to participate in the operation.

The employee took some time to actualize the plan. Obviously, there were connections and complicated issues to arrange on the outside. Finally, maybe two months after settling the agreement to participate, the employee placed a little piece of blue soap into Garino's hands, he passed it to Augusto, and Augusto to Virgolino. Virgolino found it relatively easy to take advantage of a brief moment of distraction on the guard's part to leave the soap in the prisoner's cell.

"Did you deliver it to him?" Augusto wanted to know.

"Deliver it? No, I didn't deliver it," Virgolino answered. "I left it for him in his cell."

"He won't see it," Augusto worried.

The doubt and worry lasted many weeks.

Until one day, when Virgolino placed the mess tray in the cell, the prisoner in isolation put a little piece of soap similar to what he had been given in Virgolino's pocket.

Virgolino passed it to Augusto, Augusto to Garino, and Garino to the employee.

After a few days, when he came into the workshop, he said to Garino, "Everything's okay."

Another few days later, meeting Augusto, Garino told him glowingly, "He's still locked up, but he's not alone anymore!"

Viseu's Crime is Cleared Up

Viseu's case was, in the end, far different from how everyone saw it. The court itself was tricked—and made a mistake. For years, Viseu never told anyone what had really happened. Until that day. Perhaps because that day, regaining consciousness after an attack of vertigo that knocked him out, he believed death was finally knocking on his door. Maybe, too, because Silvino had always spared a kind word for him over these long years. For one reason or another, he told him everything, but by fits and starts, as he could speak only with difficulty.

No, he, Viseu, did not commit the crime. It was his brother. On that day, at nightfall, by mere chance, he saw him walking on a byway leading out of town, which he found strange. Hobbling and afraid, he followed him through bush and forest. Up ahead, he saw him arguing with someone in the shadows, whom he didn't get to see. Viseu didn't capture the words, but the tone, though contained, was angry. Suddenly, he heard two shots and the thump of a body. In the dark, a tiny flame shone over the fallen man's face. To see if he was still alive? And then his brother fled, almost within Viseu's reach as he escaped.

Over the next few days, he began spying on his brother. He saw that he took off for the hills, and surprised him just as he was burying the pistol in a remote spot.

Viseu uncovered no explanation for the case, but neither did he look for one. His great fear was that they would discover it was his brother. What would become of his family and that flock of kids?

Everything was quiet until the day the agent appeared in the tavern displaying the lighter and asking if anyone knew who owned it. When he heard of it, Viseu felt a jolt in his heart. He recalled that little flame close to the ground the night of the crime, and he remembered that his brother had an expensive lighter of a handsome bright yellow, exactly the color of the one the agent showed at the tavern. If the investigation were to continue, they'd wind up discovering the truth.

The brother was the lifeblood of the family. As for himself, he felt useless, simply dead weight. He didn't stop to think, but acted quickly and so successfully that conviction was assured.

Catalan's New Projects

People started seeing Catalan once again going back and forth to the offices of the prison director and the social assistant.

333 buttonholed him one time on his way. "So, señor engineer, how is it passing?" he asked in a mix of Portuguese and Spanish, bowing respectfully. "Much pleasure seeing you of health. I lament what happened to you in times. If God wills, you will have more luck next."

333 was one of the few companions in prison in whom Catalan trusted. "Listen, friend of mine," Catalan answered. "Things are well on the way. I'm going to dedicate myself now to investigating the cure for cancer."

"Seriously?!" 333 tried to fake his surprise.

"Of course, seriously!"

"Well, I am sure that this time God will be at your side, señor engineer."

"He will be for sure."

They stood for another moment looking at each other face to face, Catalan with his bloated features and 333 with his sharp lines, and in both of them a pair of lively, conspiratorial eyes.

"Goodbye for now if God wills, señor engineer."

"Hasta la vista, amigo mío."

Each went on his way—333 distributing his meager milk deliveries, Catalan to speak with the director.

There was No Reason for Shock

Cumbersome and halting of step, but secure in his movements thanks to his long history as a seaman, 402 went up to Garino as they crossed paths, stopped for a second and gave him the news. "For your information, they put Virgolino into solitary."

Then he resumed walking so a guard wouldn't notice.

Garino couldn't be sure if 402 had once seen him talking with Virgolino. He must have. For sure, he also associated this news with the fact that Virgolino was the aide on C Wing who brought mess trays to the isolated Communist on the third balcony.

Bad luck, Garino thought.

Some days later, he got to speak with Augusto the gardener and gave him the news.

"Bad luck. If Virgolino talks, we're screwed."

They analyzed the situation. They'd truly be up shit's creek if Virgolino talked or if in some other way they uncovered the linkages that had been made to deliver the little piece of soap. It wouldn't take long for the PIDE to fall all over them. More than the shock, however, they sensed the worst of it would be the severing of the newborn connection so laboriously established. And the man isolated on third balcony would suffer who knows how much more.

The next few days were tense. Virgolino remained in isolation, Parrana substituting as aide with the job of going to the Communist's cell.

A month later, Virgolino was brought back to his cell. That's when the reason for his punishment came to light. It wasn't for delivering the piece of soap. They didn't know about that, and he didn't talk. But it so happened that when Virgolino delivered the mess tray, the guard lifted the lid.

"What the hell is this?!" he asked astonished. "The mess order is rice, and you're bringing him baked cod?"

Virgolino was thrown headlong down the balcony, and the cell door slammed shut with a crash. The tray went back to the kitchen, the Communist went without lunch, and Virgolino was put in a cell and later interrogated and taken to a secret unit in the basement. He assumed responsibility for the exchange of the rice but spoke neither of Augusto nor of the little piece of soap, nor of Parrana, who had offered his cod.

Days later, with cells on the whole wing all locked up, Ernesto, the guard on duty, opened Virgolino's door and came right to the point.

"You guys lucked out. Your mistake was taking us for fools. The first time I found you out was more than a year ago. But for my part, I let it pass. I also don't think it's right to keep a man isolated like that for all those years without being able to eat what he likes, same as any of you guys. Just don't think you were doing a good deed. I didn't care. But this time Rinaldo was on duty, and Rinaldo, as you know, sees everything and excuses nothing."

Weeks later, Augusto ran into Virgolino and learned what happened. He looked him in the eye and held his friend's arm for a moment. "That's people for you."

But Virgolino had another piece of news to offer. "What I did," he said in a subdued voice, "Parrana can continue doing. I know him well and I trust him."

One More Christmas Among Many

Christmas that year was the same as always. A few prisoners less, a few more. Presents from the families according to their means and their cost. As ever, the expectation, the hustling and excitement for those who had visitors, and the disappointment, bitterness or indifference for the great majority who didn't.

Every visitor a case. Every case a situation. Every situation a conversation. So very many that if the walls, the glass and the bars on the visiting booths had memory, it would be difficult for them to retain them all.

Two of them, perhaps, they would never forget.

Once again, Porto Alto was distracted from his mother's visit by the murmured conversation in the next booth between 101 and his daughter, the only one who visited him because the rest of the family had cut their ties.

After his mother's visit ended, Porto Alto's ears sharpened.

"You're always sad, father. Don't keep punishing yourself about it," the girl said in her soft, sweet voice. "What's past is past."

And as she was leaving, "I'll be back next month. Please, don't beat yourself up, father."

As he was every year, Viseu was also called to the visiting room. He went, stumbling, his body shaking, his bum arm swaying. As in past years, his whole family was in the visiting booth, brother and his wife, sons and the daughter, almost all grown up now, enveloping him in loving words that could barely be heard through the double panes and grates but that collectively sounded like a tender embrace. Viseu responded with his stammering voice. His deformed, fading face in the shadows reflected his emotions of happiness.

Silvino and Garino happened to meet that day in the corridor, where they could see the guards searching the visitors.

Silvino had discovered something new that he'd never seen before on the cell wall up under the high windows. For a long time, dozens of cocoons had pocked the faded ochre plaster with tiny black dots, and from those little round holes, small, mysterious worms emerged. Silvino was going to speak to Garino about his recent discovery when Garino called his attention to the procession of arriving visitors.

Viseu's family group was unique for the number of people, for all the youngsters among them and for their patent joyfulness.

Silvino had kept secret Viseu's revelation about the crime for which he was convicted. That day, however, owing to the deep trust he held in Garino, he told him the whole story.

Garino exploded. "What? This can't be. A man cannot stay here his whole life for a crime he didn't commit."

Immediately he proposed to Silvino that the two of them should seek out the director or go to Prison Services.

Silvino coolly shook his head. "That's the worst we could do. We'd destroy the man's happiness. Crippled as he is, he'd always be helpless. He'd have a miserable existence living off charity or at the expense of others. Saving his family is what gave his life meaning. You may think it's nonsense, but when I look at him, I think there are saints in this world and he's one of them."

Garino was not prepared to be persuaded so quickly by his sage friend. He still protested. "And his brother? And his family? How could they accept such sacrifice?"

Silvino could not find an answer to these questions. Assuming Viseu's brother and his family shared the same understanding he himself had, he said no more, as though he preferred not to think about it any further. But it didn't work. Later, in his cell, he asked himself the same question. Garino's question kept tormenting him over and over, but his doubt did not make him change his mind.

Five Hundred Stories, Only One Story

Over the long years, 402 was transferred back and forth from his cell to the infirmary for a few days' recuperation. His leg wound, resulting from his jump to the street when he tried escaping eight years before, never healed. It remained open and infected, enormous, deep, purple and always bloody. Right next to the bone, it looked like the cruel teeth marks of a wild animal. When the wound became aggravated and he couldn't move, they carried him to the infirmary. After a few days, he could walk lamely and heavy-footed and, still in the infirmary, he could go out to the garden for daily recreation. He'd seat himself on the low dividing wall in the garden and talk with whoever came to seek out his company. He aged rapidly and, suffering from degenerative arthritis, a rumbling cough and panting breath, it was hard to recognize the young seaman from a dozen years ago, when he was sentenced.

In those short perches outside of his wing, he always found moments to talk with Augusto the gardener. Though infrequent, a certain continuity informed their conversations.

It had been eight years since 402 attempted his escape, failing at the last minute by falling and smashing his leg. There was no hope to be salvaged out of his ruined leg. But in all this time, he still tried to instill Augusto with hope.

"If I had your legs, I sure wouldn't still be here," he insisted. "You can circulate through the infirmary garden and the vegetable patch. You get close to the walls without anyone suspecting you. You've already gone to the guards' quarters. With a little courage, you could get out."

Augusto did not feel inclined to follow the advice. "And if I escaped, what then? Where would I go? What would I do? I'd spend the rest of my life running, or they'd catch me again and then I'd just come back and rot here. I've already been here twelve years. I have six more to go. It's still a lot, but then I'll be able to go back home to my family and I can start living again."

They hadn't noticed another prisoner listening in, a young lad who had recently come to the penitentiary. They saw him listening, his dark eyes shining attentively.

"What do you want?" 402 demanded. "You have something to say?"

"I heard you talking, and I've thought about it," the lad said, quite full of himself. "Believe me, they won't have me here very long." Then he walked away.

"With that much willpower, he just might be telling the truth," 402 smiled.

They continued talking when 333 passed by, walking quickly with his pitcher of milk to distribute to the sick. Augusto recalled 333's unusual case: robbing his business partners and when they called him a thief, he shot them both dead in defense of his honor. "Some story," he summed up.

402 thought for a while, then spoke. From what he said, you could tell he had reflected long upon it. "His is one of the five hundred stories buried in the tomb of living beings that is this house. One of five hundred."

"Each one has his own," Augusto sighed.

"For some here, prison is an episode of their life," 402 continued. "It's a part of it. It's connected to it, and sometimes without it, the rest of their life makes no sense. I'm here for the rest of my life just on account of one second of my life. One second, nothing more. It happened. But it might not have happened."

He paused, then went on. "In the end, my story is my whole life spent here. The way things stand now, I won't be leaving."

"Life's not over," Augusto consoled him.

They were silent a few beats.

"You know what else?" 402 picked up the thread. "There's every-thing here. Some of us are better than others, but we're all human beings. If you're talking about stories, there are two kinds of stories. The five hundred different stories of us five hundred prisoners who are here now. Each one a story that begins and a story that ends."

He paused again, then went on. "And there's the story that has no end, a single story, the story of this place, these walls, the grates, the cells, the isolation cages, through which have passed not just the five hundred of us here now, but the thousands and thousands who have gone through."

One Day More, One Day Less

That day, like every day, week after week, month after month, year after year, life unfolded in its infinite ritual.

The night silence pierced by the dawn whistles and the sudden expansion of sound as the prison came alive. The noisy, cadenced opening of locks and bolts on the cells, one after another. The slap of the aides' sandals circulating with the buckets of human waste. The metallic bang when the buckets were thrown on the cement floor. The smell oozing throughout the wings mixed with and covered by disinfectant. More whistles, lineups, countdowns. The distribution of coffee and bread crusts. The lines of men off to the workshops. More locks and bolts, now with renewed slamming of doors and isolation inside the solitary cells. Then the dying down of sounds and the enlarging vacuum of the wings' immensity, interrupted only by the unpredictable rhythms of the aides' clogs and slippers, the sound of hammering, sawing and machines coming from the workshops.

Midday and the spread of nauseating smells—the mustiness of kale soup and fish fried in rancid oil infusing the viscous humidity of the air, the ground, the walls, everything. Lunch and renewed animation and repetition of sounds and movements. And once again, the roll call; and then again, the relative silence. And once again, the loud opening of cell doors, another lineup and parade down to recreation. Another lineup, another roll call, all afternoon another repetition of movements, relocations, sounds and dinner smells.

And as always, at the end of the day, the lineup in the wings for the count-off, everyone at his cell door. As always, the guards' whistles, the closing in for the night and the insistent sound of a series of closing locks and bolts. More than five hundred prisoners, more than five hundred cells. And finally, the great rotunda hall, with the slamming down of its own unique grate.

On that day, as on so many others, as companion to the progressive darkening, the cold and humidity invaded the vast wings, filtering into the cells, as if sticking to the cement and iron of the very structure. As usual, during the hour of silence, the sounds gradually diminished. And feebly breaking the atmosphere, Old Man's eternal supplication: "Forgive me, Lord! Forgive me!"

Barely discernible, coming from another cell, 210's murmured calculation: "Thirteen years, three months and ten days; nine years, eight months and twenty days to go."

Except for the change of numbers, the litany was the same as all the others he had chanted hundreds of times for the last thirteen years. Though this time, there was something different in it. Instead of the word "still" that he always used until now, he said "to go" for the first time since he had begun counting. The phrase escaped, he didn't know why. He noticed it right away. The lapse in his tone of self-confident pride, with which he generally recited his count, left him with an unexpected shock of reflection, as if for the first time he was appraising the years he had spent there and, above all, the many he would yet spend. But in the six-pointed star's enormousness, who could guess what was going on in the soul of that single locked-up prisoner in his cell amongst the five hundred cells where five hundred prisoners were locked up alone?

And the sounds that extinguish little by little. And the silence of the advancing night.

Parrana woke up startled by the clang of the rotunda grate and the sound of footsteps, locks and bolts of a cell. The flurry that he heard eight years before came to his mind, when the PIDE brought the politicals to the third balcony. Would they finally come, again in the still of the night, looking for the man who ever since then, eight years ago, was still in isolation up there? But no. The sound was not coming from the balcony.

The next day, he would learn the cause of the nighttime disturbance. The guard on his rounds, looking through the peephole of Serpentina's cell, found him hanged in the usual way: strangled by his belt from the bars on the window above.

"One more," said Benjamim, who was called in as usual because he was discreet, and because he had the physical strength to lift a dead body.

* * *

That very same day, a woman holding her son by the hand sauntered by out on the sidewalk past the front façade. It was the first time they had walked there. The boy looked curiously up at the majestic building, the towers of white stone, the elegant trim on the battlements.

"Mother, what's this?"

"I don't know, son," the mother answered. "It must be the palace of some rich man."

"Mother, how come the windows have bars?"

"I don't know, son," the mother answered. "Maybe because there's a lot of treasures inside and they're afraid thieves could break into the palace and steal them."

"Ah!" the boy said in wonderment. He was going to ask another question, but an electric tram rattled by just then, making such a noise that the boy kept quiet and then didn't ask his question.

Perhaps it was just as well—because maybe the mother wouldn't have known what to answer.

Author Biography

Manuel Tiago

MANUEL Tiago was the pen name of Álvaro Cunhal. Edições Avante! in Lisbon, has published nine titles by Manuel Tiago: *Até amanhã, camaradas* (Until Tomorrow, Comrades), which was adapted as a Portuguese television series in 2005; *A estrela de seis pontas* (The Six-Pointed Star); *A Casa de Eulália* (The House of Eulália); *Fronteiras* (Border Crossings); *Um risco na areia* (A Line in the Sand); *Os corrécios e outros contos* (The Slackers and Other Stories); *Sala 3 e outros contos* (The 3rd Floor and Other Stories); and *Lutas e vidas* (Struggle and Life). *Cinco dias, cinco noites* (Five Days, Five Nights), adapted to film in 1996, was the first of his works of fiction to appear in English (International Publishers, 2020).

Álvaro Cunhal was born in Coimbra, Portugal, on November 9, 1913. He began his revolutionary activity as a student at the law school (Faculdade de Direito) of Lisbon. He participated in the student movement and was elected in 1934 as the student representative to the University Senate. He was a militant in the Federation of Portuguese Communist Youth (Federação da Juventude Comunista Portuguesa), and was elected its secretary-general in 1935. In that year he went underground and participated in Moscow in the Sixth International Communist Youth Congress. He joined the Portuguese Communist Party (Partido Comunista Português, PCP) in 1931.

Arrested in 1937 and 1940, and subjected to torture, he returned to political struggle as soon as he was freed after several months in prison. He participated in the reorganization of the PCP in 1940-41. Again living clandestinely, he was a member of the party Secretariat from 1942 to 1949.

Arrested anew in 1949 and brought before a fascist court, he delivered a ringing denunciation of the fascist dictatorship and a defense of his party's program. Judged guilty, he remained for 11 years in fascist prisons, almost eight of them in complete isolation. On January

3, 1960, he escaped from the prison fortress at Peniche together with a group of brave communist militants. Once again called to the Secretariat of the Central Committee, he was elected Secretary General of the PCP in 1961.

Living abroad, in Moscow and Paris, from that time forward he participated in numerous congresses and gatherings with communist parties and other revolutionary forces in international conferences. He played a critical role in organizing worldwide support, especially within the socialist countries, for the independence movements in the far-flung Portuguese colonies in Africa.

After the downfall of the fascist dictatorship on April 25, 1974, he served as Minister without Portfolio in the first, second, third and fourth provisional governments, and was elected as a deputy to the Constituent Assembly in 1975 and to the Assembly for the Republic in 1975, 1979, 1980, 1983, 1985 and 1987. He was a member of the Council of State from 1982 to 1992.

In accordance with the decisions made at the Fourteenth Congress of the PCP in 1992 concerning renewal and a new structure of leadership, he stepped down as Secretary General of the PCP and was elected by the Central Committee as President of the National Council of the party.

In December 1996, the Fifteenth Congress of the PCP eliminated the National Council of the party and its presidency. Cunhal was re-elected as a member of the Central Committee.

He was re-elected to the Central Committee at the Sixteenth and Seventeenth party congresses in December 2000 and November 2004 respectively.

Under his own name Cunhal published several books about politics. He was a gifted artist as well: A book of his collected drawings has appeared. In addition, he published an original translation of Shakespeare's *King Lear*.

He died at the age of 91 on June 13, 2005. His funeral in Lisbon was attended by half a million people. He had one daughter, Ana Cunhal.

About the Translator

ERIC A. Gordon, a Los Angeles resident since 1990, is a native of New Haven, Connecticut. His undergraduate degree is from Yale University, where he majored in Latin American Studies. He studied Spanish five years and Portuguese two years. He also took a summer residency in Portuguese at New York University. He went on to Tulane University, where he continued studying Portuguese and wrote a master's thesis on the opera in Rio de Janeiro in the 19th century, using original sources uncovered in the Arquivo Nacional. He earned a doctorate in history, also from Tulane, writing his dissertation about the anarchist movement in Brazil in the pre-World War I era. He also studied Portuguese language and culture under a Gulbenkian Foundation fellowship in Lisbon.

International Publishers initiated its Manuel Tiago series in 2020 with Gordon's translation of *Five Days, Five Nights*.

Gordon is the author of *Mark the Music: The Life and Work of Marc Blitzstein*, and co-author of *Ballad of an American: The Autobiography of Earl Robinson*. A memoir in short story form that he translated from Portuguese, *Waving to the Train and Other Stories*, by Hadasa Cytrynowicz, appeared in 2013 from Blue Thread Press. In 2015 he executive produced the compact disk *City of the Future: Yiddish Songs from the Former Soviet Union*, a collection of songs composed in 1931 by Samuel Polonski to the lyrics of major Soviet Yiddish poets. He is the author of a currently unpublished political autobiography.

From 1995 to 2010, Gordon was Director of the Workmen's Circle/Arbeter Ring in Southern California. He previously worked at Social and Public Art Resource Center, helping to produce murals all around the city of Los Angeles, which gave him the experience to commission a mural at the Workmen's Circle building. He was Southern California Chapter Chair of the National Writers Union (Local 1981 UAW/AFL-CIO) for two terms. He has written for dozens of local, national, and international publications, mostly about art, music, culture, and politics. From 2014 onward, he has been a staff writer and editor for *People's World* online newspaper.

From 2006-09 Gordon took coursework toward certification as a Secular Jewish Leader, referred to in Yiddish as a *vegvayzer*. Upon graduation, he became a legal officiant certified to conduct weddings and other ceremonial functions, a role equivalent in law to a minister, priest, or rabbi. He has a similar endorsement as a Humanist celebrant for people of any background. For five years he served as a Deputy Commissioner of Civil Marriage for the County of Los Angeles, where he conducted 1500 marriages.

Gordon can be contacted at ericarthurgo@gmail.com.

Questions for Discussion

In his foreword, the translator suggests that honoring the humanity of each person may be the book's main message. Do you agree, or is there something else that stands out for you more importantly?

In the harsh environment of this prison we nevertheless see numerous acts and gestures of kindness, caring and charity. Do you recall some of them, and what meaning did these episodes have for you?

How are class and regional differences reflected in this book?

Religion comes up here in several contexts—as something of a help or a band aid, a spiritual discipline, perhaps entirely cynical or somewhere in between. Does the author depict both positive and negative sides of religion? In this regard, what do you think of the characters of Viseu and Gonçalo, neither of whom is outwardly religious?

Visitors to the prison play an important role in the book—family members and others, as well as sex workers in one case (though not what we would call "conjugal visits"). How would you compare these roles to what you know about prisons today?

There is a fair amount of sex in this book—sex for pay, sex by force and by circumstance, courtship, and discussion about sex. How do you think sex in prisons should be managed?

There is much talk today not just about prison reform, but prison abolition. What is your thinking?

The author offers several examples of "Robin Hood"-like behavior that benefited the poor, unemployed and hungry. The author shows us the prisoners' positive feelings about these incidents. What do you think about them?

Which characters were the most memorable for you, and why?

One isolated, surviving Communist plays a small role in the book, but he hovers over it like a saintly specter who engages our sympathies. He doesn't even have a name. Nor does the outside "employee" who turns up in the last few chapters to establish contact with him. How do you interpret the "namelessness" of these minor, but critical characters?

Based on what you've read, how do you think a Communist Party can function under such intensely repressive conditions? As a follow-up to this question, be sure to read some of the later novels and stories in our Manuel Tiago series, where he goes into quite granular detail about exactly that. .

Finally, do you know anyone, maybe yourself, who has been in prison? What were the circumstances, and how different from or true to this account of prison life were they?